NEVER FADE AWAY

# Never
# Fade
# Away

●

A   N O V E L

●

## William Hart

2002

FITHIAN PRESS

SANTA BARBARA, CALIFORNIA

Published by Fithian Press
A division of Daniel and Daniel, Publishers, Inc.
Post Office Box 1525
Santa Barbara, CA 93102
www.danielpublishing.com

LIBRARY OF CONGRESS CATALOGING-IN-PUBLICATION DATA
Hart, William, (date)
    Never fade away : a novel / by William Hart.
      p. cm.
    ISBN 1-56474-386-1 (pbk. : alk. paper)
    1. Vietnamese Conflict, 1961–1975—Veterans—Fiction. 2. Teacher-
student relationships—Fiction. 3. Vietnamese American women—Fiction.
4. Los Angeles (Calif.)—Fiction. 5. Students, Foreign—Fiction. 6. Remedial
teaching—Fiction. 7. English teachers—Fiction. 8. College teachers—
Fiction.  I. Title
    PS3558.A6844 N48 2002
    831.'54—dc21
                        2001003397

*For students and teachers everywhere*
*who have suffered misguided administrators*

NEVER FADE AWAY

9/3/85

Can you smell in a dream? Or did I just dream it last night?

I was eighteen again, stepping from a DC-8 into Vietnam for the first time, slugged in the face by the stench of that steaming green land. It burned in my nose and lungs like nothing I'd ever known, a composite of rotting garbage, smoke from fires, human sweat—all cooking at 115 degrees. Boy did it scare me. I was thinking, if I can't even take the smell of the place....

Woke in the wee hours to an odor equally unforgettable: the fetor of deceased human flesh curing in equatorial sun. For a long time it clogged my nostrils, even though I was awake. Ended up sleeping on the living room couch, where it seemed less. This morning it was gone.

I found it easier to enter Vietnam than ever to leave. Part of me can never leave, I guess.

Sooooo, what else?... Oh yeah. Today was the first day of fall semester. Rah rah, sis boom bah.

Dutifully administered the John Goddard Electroshock Lecture to my ENGL 002 sections. Fire and brimstone did rain down till every trembling eyeball glowed in terror. Well, they've got to know we're not convened to play pattycake. Get used to it, dudes: the zeros in English 002 signify you're in college by a vagrant hair. Shine fast or we snip you.

Christ have I got a lot of Asians in those classes. Sixty percent, I bet. Workload will be a bitch, and for my pains, at semester's end, I'll preside over yet another slaughter of the innocents. Wonder how many I can rescue this time.

Crossed my mind the Department could be stacking my rosters. Perfect way to guarantee an instructor they want to get rid of has low pass rates.

Yet I prefer another scenario, more flattering. Some of the Asians, I know, come looking for my sections. And they've got a pretty good grapevine going. Am I being screwed by my own competence?

*Tuesday, September 3*

Today is first class meeting for English 002. When teacher walk in, I am disappoint. A man teacher. I think he is 40 years old, maybe. His name is Mr. Goddard.

He make strong speech, scare us to death. He tell about final exam in December how tough it will be, how we will fail for sure if we dont be serious. Usually more than 50% fail 002, he say. Next he give worser news, if you fail any English class two time, you flunk out school, that's it buddy!

Everybody so quiet to hear those evil facts. Even the guys look scare (which we know they hate). In our little class, 15 students sit, 15 stand behind to see if they can add, all are misery. Only sound is clock running, its little finger goes around, I feel misery too.

Then Mr. Goddard talk to us more positive. Inch by inch his words rise us up from misery condition. Even if final is tough, he say, some students always pass. And if our class work hard, more can do it. Also, he promise to help us every way. He is English as Second Language teacher, his job is help student like us, etc, etc, etc.

Well, he seem sincere and I want to believe. But I remember my last semester English teacher. On first day she promise we will learn so much, then she give us only lazy teaching and many harsh judgements. In that class, all fail but three.

I must watch this new teacher. Are his words and actions same, or is he another fake one? If he is fake, I must decide some other plan to pass.

Tonight, I burn money and pray to my family. I promise my parents, my grandparents, I will pass English 002 this time. As spirits they watch me everything I do, how can I lie to them or break my swear?

In this journal I make second promise. If I fail English 002 again, flunk out school, disgrace my elder generations, I will end my shameful existence.

Signed Sincerely,
Tien Le

No way to fail English now. Because I always keep promise, and I dont wanna die.

9/4/85

Planned to finish the novel by the start of school. However…didn't happen. I guess it's not that unusual for me to miss a self-imposed deadline, but I still don't like it. Feels as though life is slipping away as I run in place. New deadline: Thanksgiving.

I'll have to stop then anyway to revise the story collection. That deadline is not flexible, being someone else's. My first book publication. Would hate to blow it.

Sometimes, when I reflect on the novel, I have to ask myself whether the world really needs my black-comic saga of the doughty Corporal Ernest Candide. One more negative, mocking book about Vietnam. Six hundred grisly pages of hopelessness, overseasoned with irony.

Well, I think so, if it's good enough.

*Thursday, September 5*

Mr. Goddard explain we must write in this diary such as following: old memories, good and bad experiences, friends and enemies, important lessons we learn, things we believe, things we want to change, and anything we observe each day and want to tell. Minimum, 5 page per week.

He say we can write about pet peeps too, but what it is I wander? I suppose he mean we can write about our animals we keep in the house, which is popular American custom. Everybody has their doggy or kitty, and they love them more than people. Which of course is easy!

Can boring person like me write 5 page per week? I think I can, I did it before.

When I was nine, I keep diary just for fun. That one my father give it for my birthday. Its American, because he get it from his American customer. It have pink plastic cover, with flowers, say MY DIARY on front. Also, there is this little lock and key so I can lock it. None of my friends have one, in Vietnam diary is a strange idea. That make mine even more special, once father explain its function.

I write in there for more than one year. Until all pages fill, then I lose the key, so I can't open. But after, I hide the diary in my chest, under blankets. I am thinking, when I grow up I buy new key, then I can open it, see how I change over the years.

Too bad that diary is lost. I leave it behind in our house with everything else the night we sneak out of Vietnam.

9/6/85

DATELINE: SOME AEGEAN ISLAND, 1100 B.C.

The stunning goddess Calypso saves Odysseus from drowning in the sea. She is quite smitten with the brave adventurer, though Homer doesn't tell us why. She installs him in her magnificently appointed cave, lavishes him with delectable foods and divine wine, reclines in his arms as the man who swam for three days does his utmost to please.

In her attempt to secure his permanent affections, Calypso offers immortality. By the contract, Odysseus will be eternally in his prime, all luxuries at his fingertips, a sweet-natured and voluptuous superwoman blazing nightly in his sack.

Yet he declines. Goddesses hold no allure for him. All day long he pines loyally on the beach, beard soggy with lonesome tears, desiring only to sail home to his wrinkling human Penelope.

UPDATE: LOS ANGELES, 1985

By light of day and dark of night Odysseus Jr. dreams of Calypso as he shacks up frustrated with his domineering muse Clementine. Perpetually he spins her sheets of written creativity, and in return she bestows no food, no drink, no sex, no immortality—just a two-buck ticket in the great sweepstakes of literary renown.

Jr. suspects his bright-eyed muse is seeing other writers on the sly, delighting in their favors as she dings them with the Wand of Genius she conceals from him, but he can't prove it.

So why does he permit her to sap his spirit, darken his pillow, cornhole his credit rating?

Love is blind, that's why. Also, she's the best he can do. Let's face it: no woman of fire has ever been able to suffer the writer's life for long. Tennis players get the Calypsos. Tennis players and hoods.

*Saturday, September 7*

When I pack this morning, I expect Mrs. Coberly to argue me one more time, but instead she offer ride, quite helpful.

I think I can like it here. Apartment is on second floor of house, another apartment across hall good for safety. Its a clean place with many windows and much light. The view is not special—just old houses, apartments. A street go by our front yard up the hill to campus.

Best thing is I have my own bedroom with nice big desk to study. And there is kitchen where I can cook my food. For all, I pay only $205, its the cheapest rent of the nine places I look. Of course, for such rent, this place is not perfect, outside some paint is come off, my window is crack, stuff like that. But I know I can't have everything, its nice enough for now.

My roommate Rayneece seem like polite and intelligent person. I believe she is trustable girl with high character, whatever Mrs. Coberly say. Rayneece graciously share her food with me tonight, because I dont have my own yet.

She is business major. She tell me all about it. In her future she will start a cosmetics company, be the boss, have her own jet and fly to meetings!

9/9/85

The most significant variable in warfare, to my way of thinking, is the in-your-face factor, the degree of hands-on engagement required to ensure the enemy's decease.

Toward the primitive end of the spectrum is the soldier who prefers to kill with a blade. He will savor the rasp of parting ribs, the pop of organs, the opponent's gurgling groan. The knifesman knows when his job is done and usually he does it well. He's in touch with his work, sometimes in love with his work. Other intimate weapons are hammers, candlesticks, garroting wires. Fingers, nails, and teeth of course represent the ultimate in intimacy, but because of their inefficiency are most often weapons of last resort.

Martial minds toward spectrum center will favor middle-range modes of attack. Odysseus chose the crossbow, much to the dismay of his wife's suitors. For me, it was a .45.

Rifles obviously are less intimate than handguns. Rockets, mortars, artillery—less intimate still.

The B-52s would come in at 30,000 feet, high above the clouds, you couldn't even hear them they were so high. But the bombs you could hear. Falling miles away they'd wake you in the middle of the night, tightly over-lapping concussions fused into one immense shuddering rumble that shook the earth. Falling closer, they became a blazing Armageddon that sucked the air right out of your chest.

Once our squad did a body count after a wall-to-wall carpet our CO called in. Fearless Leader thought he was stomping on a big enemy pow-wow, based on questionable intelligence our interrogators had beaten out of a captured VC.

We hiked five klicks through hills and jungle and in a high valley found a barren moonscape of big craters and uprooted, shattered trees. All on valley floor was levelled. The timber at valley rim, stripped of bark and leaves, leaned away from the devastation as though slapped backward by the hand of God.

We spent the afternoon combing the mass of debris for enemy kills, collecting each shard of bone and every strip of flesh, laying them on the trunk of a fallen banyan. Each bit counted as one kill.

We confirmed 32 kills, though all the pieces could have come from—and I believe did come from—one unlucky water buffalo.

Predictably, our diligence did not please our commander. Thirty-two kills to him were not enough. Had we maybe missed some? To give the man his due, he had greater goals. Like many practitioners of the long distance coup de grâce, he was never satisfied. Always shooting for a personal best.

*Tuesday, September 10*
Today I learn this diary not private! Mr. Goddard call it writing journal, say we have to turn in so he can read. On Thursday! He cant see what I write in here! What will I do!

My hard thinking on this problem reveal what I must do. I must write new journal, which I can show it to my teacher. Forget personal stuff, I will write educated things, intelligent ideas, I will impress him, make him notice and say, here is smart student who should pass my course. Tonight, after I finish physics homeworks, I will begin.

Unfortunately, because I become upset about journal, I cant concentrate on essay we write in class today. Its our first big assignment, suppose to be 500 words, all I write is one messy page. I know I fail.

Why cant I listen better in class? Did anyone else make my dumb mistake, write private diary? I doubt it. My fault is, I am let my mind wonder sometimes, I am miss what teacher say.

So stupid!

*9/11/85*
The chickens dropped in last night. It's been a while, many months. As usual, I shot their butts off. Hope they're happy.

My second nightmare involves the 002 essays written in class today. I've never seen so many ESL basket cases in my life! Christ on a crutch.

I am irredeemably fucked.

*Wednesday, September 11*

Recently I learn Rayneece character is not so high as I believe.

First, her friendly smile and polite behavior disappear. Now she ignore me, unless I do something wrong.

Plus, she let her boyfriend stay here. I dont know his name, because Rayneece didnt introduce him, even though he seem to be living in our house. They dont talk to me much, so usually I stay in my room. I begin to wander, did Rayneece act sweet before to trick me so I will live here, help pay rent?

The worse part is when they go in Rayneece room. Even though they shut the door, and I shut my door, I can hear them. Her bed rattle and they moan and groan, they dont even try to be polite.

Their noises make me remember the island, I cant help it. In my mind I go back there—I see it happen again. And if I go to sleep, I dream it.

I want to cut that stuff out of my mind. But it is there forever and can come when it wants. Often it comes when I am weak.


*9/14/85*

In the DMV last week I saw a guy who reminded me a lot of Dad—in the shape of his head. Very distinctive head, especially in the U.S.

Cezanne captures well such cabezas in his "Cardplayers," though he exaggerates slightly. The cranium is large and tall, with a straight high forehead, hawk nose, thin lips, strong square chin, smallish ears.

When Gary and I were kids, Dad told us he'd noticed the farmers in northern France had heads like his, as he marched through near the end of the war. It was a question in his mind until in Paris he met a woman who joyously informed him that our family name is as French as French bread. "Countryman!" she cried, and gave Dad a big kiss.

Gary and I were left to ponder our Frenchness, as well as the details expurgated from Pop's version of his Paris visit.

Gary has a head much like Dad's. Me, a little less. I'm not built on their massive scale generally, and when it comes to heads, I have a lower hairline, fuller lips, more tapered chin. The broken-looking beak we share.

I have scars like Dad now, but that of course has less to do with genetics than misguided family legacy. My father's principal scar runs from his right shoulder to his left hip, an inch wide in the middle, tapering at the ends. Whenever we pulled rocks, he'd take off his shirt, and it fascinated me, that nontanning white scar, as did the story behind it, always told bluntly with few details. A Luftwaffe bombardier dumped a 500-pounder in the roadside ditch where Dad was lying, and Pop lost the tussle. Almost died. Imagine, from a little thing like that.

This is the old buzzard's birthday, if he's still kicking.

*Monday, September 16*
When I fill application for work-study, I ask for technician job in computer lab. I feel my math major make me qualify, also I supervise the computer center at high school during senior year.

Lucky for me, they give what I ask. I am assign to university computer lab. Today I go to work first time.

My boss Robert is Mexican, I think, with short hairs that stand up straight on his head. He seem so serious, he's about 20 years in age.

Kindly he tell me some advice to show how ignorant I am about computers and the mistakes I will make. He's physics major, and accordingly to him, physics is the toughest major at CSUM.

What is my major, he ask.

I learn math is only third toughest major.

I dont know if working for Robert will be fun, but one good thing, I won't be ignorant about computers or anything for long. As he share his intelligence with me, I will become wise woman.

Last week, I did a stupid thing. Now it worry me a lot. When I try to write new journal to impress my teacher, it keep sounding silly to me, so finally I pick up one of Rayneece magazine and look inside. One story interest me. It concern how black ladies go bald because they tie their hair in knots.

That give me idea, I decide to write a report and warn black ladies: dont tie your hair in that manner. Thus, I can use some of the ideas in the story, but say them in my own words.

I sit down, prepare to write. I find I dont know how to start. I sit many minutes, thinking, nothing seem to happen in my head. I did not sleep the night before, so I am very tire. I have terrible headache and I see little white spots.

I look in the magazine to understand how the writer begin. I like the way she begin very much. So I borrow her sentence.

Well, I try to say her ideas with my words. But each time I look in magazine it seem like she say the ideas so much better than me. I start to copy the story, not change much.

When I finish, I copy another story same way, and soon I have 14 page total, more than enough. In my sleepy head, I tell myself the extra pages make up for copying.

Now I wander, will my teacher catch me? Will he see I cheated?

9/17/85
The death smell returned last night. Woke me again. This time I was able to recall some of the dream that went with it.

I'm swimming on a sea, no land in sight. My body's tired, but I can't quit swimming. To quit is oblivion. On and on I stroke, losing power slowly as I run out of gas.

I sense a presence somewhere beneath me. It watches my struggle, waiting. I feel if I quit swimming, I will sink to it, and it will have me.

End of dream.

My nightmares get more surreal over time, more threatening too. And what am I to make of dream content leaking into real life?

DIAGNOSIS: The boy's head is sorely fucked, M'lord. 'Twould be kindness to amputate.

TREATMENT: Anodynes of choice in hair-raising quantities.

PROGNOSIS: Abandon hope ye who enter here.

*Tuesday, September 17*

Mr. Goddard give back our first essay today, and mine has NC grade, mean No Credit—Fail. Even though I expect this, but my stomach get sick anyway.

He return our journals too, everybodys but mine. Mine he keep it on his hand, tell me please see him after class. Then he put it on his desk.

Later, when he write on board, I sneak out of the room. I dont think he saw.

I know he's gonna tell me I cheat my journal, therefore I fail the course. And I want to avoid. But of course I avoid nothing by sneak out of class. If he want to fail me, I can only delay his action.

Too late to change teachers. What will I do?

Naturally Rayneece pick tonight to yell at me because of my showers. She say I make big water bill, one shower per day is enough for any person, dont you realize we live in a dam desert, she accuse. Her attitude is quite rude. She lecture me like auntie teach the little girl.

I decide I will take my showers when she's not here. No more than three per day, that way I will avoid conflict with this unreasonable, selfish, and insulting person. I did not bother to mention that she and her boyfriend keep me awake last night, *again*. She should think of stuff like that before she criticize my showers.

*9/18/85*

MHP asked why I haven't turned in her frigging surveys. Told her they'd been dutifully administered, right on schedule, but somebody broke into my car and stole them.

The look on her face was priceless. She knew I was lying, but what could she do?

Yeah, her survey. She wants our foreign-born students to translate ten English sentences into their first languages. Looks innocent enough. But what are the odds? In some way or other she's going to skew the data, drawing her own foregone conclusions in order to fuck over students and instructors too. Her M.O. never varies.

It's a byproduct of her warped nature. Just as scorpions love to sting, More Humping Power craves the hump. Three times a year, with her nightmare finals, she happily humps all writing students. She humps us teachers too, as we try to do our impossible jobs while dancing in the gears of her Kafkan torture machine.

Screw the Empress of Decomposition! May Mary Hughes Parcell meet the thrill of her life on the business end of an impaling spike.

Environmental footnote: the surveys were not wasted. They were recycled to my stock of scratch paper. Just wish I'd thought to ask old Hump for more surveys—to replace the stolen ones. Can't get enough of that there scratch paper. Know what I mean?

*Thursday, September 19*

For two days I can't sleep, cant eat because of weak stomach, worry all the time. Finally I visit Mr. Goddard in his office before class. I confess what I did: copy magazine, cheat my journal.

His reaction surprise me. There is no lecture, he just ask me to explain why I do it. So I tell him about this diary, about why he cant read it—and about the new journal I try to write all in one night.

He give no punishment for cheating, nothing. He just say, don't do it again. And, to my shock, he tell me I can keep writing in this diary for my journal assignment! He wont read it because its too personal, he will only count the pages. However, I must do three page more per week than the other students because my assignment is special.

When I leave his office, I am very happy, I am thinking he is so kind. He can fail me—but instead he give special assignment. What a nice teacher!

Then, I begin to wander. Why is he so nice and easy? Already he treat me different from others in my class. Does he want something? I hate to be ungrateful person, but I know many Americans wear one face outside, second face inside. Always wise to be careful.

*9/19/85*

There are many different reasons for plagiarism, some founded on the gravest academic sins, some justifiable.

The most perceptive student of English literature I know admitted to me that she plagiarized written assignments during her first term at Oxford. By this unorthodox means she trained herself to read and write English (her second language) with the proficiency of her British classmates. She then dumped the crutch, flying unassisted in her adopted tongue. Cribbing as a learning tool.

Obviously, not all plagiarism is equally constructive. It depends on context, motive, the degree of sincerity involved. I really let a student off the hook today. I did it because she was honest with me about her reasons. Time will tell whether I made a mistake.


*Saturday, September 21*

Since two days I do not see Rayneece, even at night she is gone. At first I feel so peaceful with her and the boyfriend not here. I dont have to hide in my room, I can watch TV, cook my food, anything I want. Also I dont have to listen to their sex noises.

But after dark sometimes I get nervous. I know this isn't safest neighborhood. One time Rayneece warn me dont walk alone at night, always lock the door, lock windows when you leave.

But are locks enough? Can't the criminal break in? And what if he has knife or gun? How I will protect myself? It can be very bad, as I imagine.

With all the lights off it's so scary in this old house!


*9/22/85*

Eddie's dead. Been seeing it on the news since yesterday evening. His dad called this morning.

Wanted to fly back for the funeral, but Mr. P. talked me out of it. Says I should wait and visit next summer, when things have settled. At this point, everybody's just trying to figure out what happened.

His father's as much in the dark as me. All we know is how he died. He tried to stick up a bank yesterday and ended up in a two-hour firefight with a Boston SWAT unit. Inexplicable, but those are the facts.

Here's the one guy we were sure had come through it all relatively unfazed, even though he'd seen more than his share. When I visited him in Lynn a year ago he seemed great to me, better than ever. It was a rainy fall day. We drank beer in his den, vaguely watched the Notre Dame football team pound somebody, had some laughs. Only change I saw was a little gray hair.

Eddie loved his wife (I'm sure of that), and his kids are about the nicest I've ever met. He always seemed satisfied with his job, though not ecstatic—who is? Making good money; no bad habits that I know. If he gambled, I never heard of it.

The guy really had it all, if anyone did. Just doesn't compute. Bitter confusing knowledge.

When I am old and my brain cells are winking out like ancient stars, the memory I may retain longest is of Eddie and me on that cathouse balcony in Saigon, pissing into the staff general's jeep, laughing so hard we almost fell in our toilet. Not easy to aim, when you're laughing.

Then there was that night in the Ho Bo Woods when Eddie went with us to bring in the wounded sentry. It was our job, not his. But we wouldn't have made it back without him. He got four kills—something he didn't need or want.

Edward James Pendergrass, the Rock, laid to rest in his prime, having lived about three full lives in half a lifetime.

Boy do I feel like shit tonight. Screw the goddamn universe.


*Tuesday, September 24*
In English, our new paper assignment is tell about something that happen to you or that you witness.

At first I think such paper will not be difficult. I decide to tell about life in Can Tho when the communist come. I remember clearly because its so awful, I find I have much to say.

All weekend, between other homeworks, I write my rough draff. By Sunday night I have 11 pages, and still I am not finish. Surely there is problem. Who ever hear of English 002 paper with 11 or more pages? I decide to wait and ask my teacher if I am doing something wrong.

After class, I go to him. His face is surprise to see so many pages, but he read them all—very fast. Then he look at me and ask, you want to tell about the communist takeover in Can Tho?

When I shake my head yes, he explain I can't tell everything, I have to choose a small part, use it to show big picture.

That kind of make sense, but I don't know what part to choose. I leave, walk to cafeteria for lunch, and on the way it hit my mind what to write. I will tell about my brother and his friend Dao, what the communist did to them. So many ideas jump in my head it seem like I arrive to cafeteria in just one minute.

Strangely, Mr. Goddard say he was in Can Tho—in 1969, when he was soldier. I guess it's possible, but I dont know. We see few Americans where I live. In 1969, I was 7.


9/26/85

On the walk to school today, as I came down the last long hill before campus, three skateboarders flashed past me on the street doing about 40, bare-torsoed, glowing with life.

That's what we were like at that age, if memory serves. Reckless, cocksure, independent, innocent, scared maybe, but tough enough not to show it. Backed by buddies, drunk with the heady hubris of youth, we were just beginning to open our puppy eyes to the enormity of life.

So many adults, over time, slip into the semi-comfortable, carefully circumscribed lives that kill dreams, then personalities. Even the bravest and most ambitious are often ground down by life's gears. In defeat many lose the faith, sinking into hypocrisy, brownnosing, dirty politics, the spiderwebs of self-deceit. Over time they become ghouls of the human spirit, dead in the midst of life, alienated from their own existences. Thoreau knew them. They are the men who "lead lives of quiet desperation."

Most young people haven't sold out. That's their secret. They still see value in being themselves. And I say more power to those selves. My god, what a stinking pisspot society would be without them. Their only problem is they're already infected with the disease that will one day snuff their sparks: maturation.

*Friday, September 27*

Rayneece come back yesterday, but she dont stay. She take some clothes and makeups, then leave, without say one word.

I watch through window. She walk to her boyfriends car, get in, they drive away.

Why she rent this apartment if she dont want to use it? I worry she will move in with boyfriend, then who will share the rent with me? It is due October 3. If I must pay it all myself, I cant afford.

*9/28/85*

"The squeaking wheel gets the grease" is often true in practice, but usually a bad idea, sometimes tragedy. You wouldn't want to follow it in triage, for instance, because the patient making the loudest noise is rarely the worst hurt.

On college campuses the axiom doesn't work either. Wealthy and middle-class students are quick to squeak about any perceived problem, though on the whole they encounter few. Squeaking comes naturally to the privileged. They all know how to do it loud and long, individually and in packs. For them it is a romantic form of social mixing and a mate browse. With their confident squeaks, backed by affluent parents and the best lawyers, rich students grab just about all the grease there is to grab.

By contrast, poor students and ones with foreign accents rarely squeak in a way that can be heard by the powerful. In part that's because the powerless know a certain fact much better than the rest of us: a squeak can get you stomped on.

Many of our students learned squeaklessness in the underfunded public schools of East L.A. Others on small farms in Mexico or

Guatemala. Others as members of oppressed minorities (or majorities) back in Cambodia, Laos, Vietnam, Soviet Armenia, El Salvador, Nicaragua. Others as economic refugees from Hong Kong, Korea, Taiwan, China, the Phillipines, Indonesia, Malaysia, Burma, Bangladesh, India.

The polyglot students of CSUM are quiet but tough, and their toughness is that of the ancient peasant—a leatherlike durability cured to absorb 10,000 blows without a flinch or whimper. Sadly, this near-heroic squeaklessness is the root of our whole fucking problem! Cal State, Maravilla needs squeaking most desperately, like no other campus I know. Throughout our corrupt little kingdom, after squeakfree decades of neglect, many wagons are broken and rotting, many axles ready to snap. The grease is all being shipped elsewhere, man.

And we're a state school. So pitiful it is.

*Monday, September 30*
After two weeks in computer lab, I know my job and how to answer most questions. Often Robert is able to study at his desk while I take charge.

I don't mind, I like to keep busy. Also I know Robert must study hard to succeed in number one toughest major. However, when I consider how easy I make it for him, his immature behavior today bothers me.

He criticise me harshly, in front of other people, because I allow this grad student to save two chapters of her thesis on the hard drive. The reason I did it is because I can not sell her floppy disc. And that's because Robert take supply cabinet key when he go to lunch, like always.

"We're not bookstore," he say. "She knows she has to save. Why doesn't she bring a floppy?"

"Our policy is sell floppy to those who need."

He ignore. Instead he describe the terrible things will happen if everybody save on hard drive when they want. He make it sound like whole building fall down.

"If your so worry about the hard drive," I ask, "why do you save video games in there?" He have about 10 games saved, and I never see him play.

But he just order me delete the chapters.

I must obey, but first I save the ladys data on my floppy, so I can give to her. As I clean the hard drive I want to delete Robert's video games too, but I dont. I refuse to be a baby like him. Life will teach him.

*10/1/85*

Can't get Eddie off my mind, though it's been more than a week since he died. Part of the process, I suppose.

In his passing there's no big fear for me, I think, no handwriting on the wall. Just personal loss. Great personal loss.

Eddie's the one guy I thought would always be there.

*Wednesday, October 2*

In Student Union today I see Duc. He see me too, but ignore.

I meet Duc last fall, calculus class, he sit next to me from first day. Later, we are in same study group. Duc invite me to join because all are his friends. They are guys and girls, all Vietnamese, all major in math or engineering or computer science. Of course I say yes because study group very helpful for homeworks, and bestest way for having friends. This is what I think.

Unfortunately, everybody in that group act funny. The guys like to joke with me, but when we talk about math, they put me down. The girls put me down anyway. I study with them for some weeks. But I am not comfortable with them as they are to each other.

The reason I stick to them is because Duc treat me nice, he is the one always share answers on our math assignment. And when the group go bowling, Duc invite me too.

At first, when I roll the ball, it bump down loud on the floor, make everybody turn and look. Duc notice I am embarrass, show me how to roll it with only a little bump. With his somewhat patient teaching, I begin to push down some pins, not roll in ditch every time. And he give me praise, which make me happy. Doesn't matter what others think if Duc is my friend.

Then Duc and me are away from study group sometimes. We walk, go to park or restaurant. One day in the restaurant he tell me all about his family leaving Vietnam. They are the lucky ones, they leave on American airplane 3 weeks before capture of Saigon. They lose home and property of course, but keep their lives. Also, they bring gold to America, use it to buy a grocery over here.

As I listen to his story, I begin to worry. I feel he will expect me to say how I leave Vietnam. That is too personal for our level of friendship.

When it is my turn, I decide to tell him a little, keep the rest secret. I say my family and me leave on a boat, get in big storm, and my parents die. I dont say how they die, and I leave out the pirates.

When I finish, Duc don't ask no questions. I think he notice I am uncomfortable. I believe he is sensitive. Which increase my respect for him.

Later, we go to his car in parking lot. Other days he will start the car before I close my door. But that day he wait and wait. He say this and that, make no sense. Suddenly he grab me, I feel his hand on my leg. I think he try to kiss me too, I'm not sure.

I push him away and yell, Quit it! I realize there are many cars in the parking lot but no people.

He stop grabbing me. He say, Dont act so pure.

That make me see whats in his mind. Of course he figure out what happen to me. I am dirty, he decide, I am not the girl he can take home to meet his family. But maybe he can have fun with me. What does it matter, girl like me. When I remember how he look at me, even today I feel such shame.

I get out of his car and go back in restaurant. I phone cab to take me home. Duc come and beg me go with him, promise he wont touch me, but I ignore. Finally he get mad and leave.

Back home, I throw up. I have this bad taste wont go away. I brush my teeth, wash my mouth with mouthwash, take long shower, rub my skin with brush. I rub everywhere. My skin is burn but I still rub and rub.

I quit study group after that. When I walk past them in library, they smile and say things I cant quite hear. I keep my head high, refuse to take their level. On the calculus final, the top score is mine, without their help. I think I win in the end.

Today, when I see Duc in Union, my hate is gone. But my skin burn and bad taste come in my mouth! Why I dont know.

Here is good news: Rayneece visit. She stay only two hours, but she give me check for rent. Now I know we live here one more month at least!

*10/4/85*

A few weeks ago I let a student off on a plagiarism rap. Wasn't sure I did the right thing.

Now she's written one of the brightest rough diamonds I've ever received from a student—and it's not that rough. Just needs a little development here, a little trimming there. Some work on verbs and sentence structure.

It was the narrative assignment that got her going. She tells what happened when her older brother Minh fell in love with Dao Vuong, whose father was the communist block leader for their neighborhood in Can Tho. Dao loved Minh too, and they wanted to get married, but her parents opposed.

Mr. and Mrs. Vuong pointed out to their daughter that Minh wasn't from a "revolutionary family." Didn't she remember that during the war Minh's father sold electrical supplies to the American construction companies? Was it her desire to tarnish the Vuong family name by whelping little imperialist running dogs? Had she forgotten her heritage—a noble clan of street sweepers stretching back into the mists of time?

According to the Vuongs, the Les were worthless, all of them, from the condescending grandfather right down to the spoiled bourgeois brats. Who were the Les anyway, now that Uncle Ho had confiscated their business and most of their property? Dao was forbidden to see Minh or speak to him. Her parents began looking for a suitable communist bridegroom.

The lovers, headstrong individually, more so together, did something quite foolhardy in that time and place. They eloped. They planned to flee the country on a boat, but the night of their escape they were picked up by the Can Tho police and held for violating curfew.

Trying to protect each other during interrogation both refused to talk, and so they were beaten. It wasn't until the next night when Mr. Vuong reported his daughter missing that the police put two and two together. Dao was released immediately. Minh remained in jail another week, receiving daily martial payments from the cops for the trouble they'd got into for roughing up the daughter of a party functionary.

Minh was still recovering from the beatings when he was drafted into the Vietnamese army. After training, he was sent to the front in Cambodia—a death sentence, as everyone knew. It was assumed that Mr. Vuong had pulled strings. A block leader had the power, and the timing left little doubt.

Not long after, Mr. and Mrs. Le received a form letter from the government stating their son had died in action defending the People's Democracy near some village in Cambodia. Being realists, the Les had prepared for this news and accepted it fairly well.

Dao was prepared too. The morning she heard, she tried to kill herself with hoarded codeine pills. Her parents found her passed out and had her stomach pumped. When they brought her home from the clinic, they put her to bed. Sometime during the night she snuck out of the house. My student believes she went to the park by the river where she and Minh used to meet in secret, hold hands, and watch the boats go by. Some days later, the coast guard found her body miles downriver, weighed down by several layers of clothes.

The paper is a narrative, in line with the assignment, but it has the quality, structure and emotional power of a short story. The characters, dialogue, description are just right—and although the writer's emotions are everywhere, the tone is matter of fact, almost flat. That contrast develops a powerful tension. I really do think if she revised carefully she could publish it as a story.

I'm so proud of her. This could be exactly the success she needs to find her way in 002, and in English for that matter. It's like the novice quarterback making the football spiral for the first time. All else follows from that one miracle.

I mean, I don't doubt she's written well in Vietnamese or Chinese before. Skill like hers doesn't come out of nowhere. But to do it in English—whole new ball game. And now she's done it.

PAPERS LIKE HERS ARE FUCKING WHY I GOT INTO TEACHING!! And now I remember why I studied ESL.


*Friday, October 4*
Often I think about my fail in English 002 last spring. How is it possible only three student pass that class?

I know one reason. My teacher assign strange and difficult papers. Seem like I always feel confuse about what to write. Example, Ms. Cowley have us write about our most significant epiphany, she call it. She think its a wonderful assignment, then she see our papers, find out nobody in class understand what epiphany mean, so we write every silly thing.

Having your purse stolen is not an epiphany, Laura, Ms. Cowley lecture one student.

It never happen to you, Laura say.

I write about a sports award I win in Vietnam, second prize in table tennis competition, but Ms. Cowley say thats not epiphany either. It must be less physical, more mental, she tell me.

Another time Ms. Cowley assign us to write a paper on the qualities that make a good teacher. Uh-oh, I realize, anything I say might sound like criticism on Ms. Cowley. So I write about my teachers in Vietnam, where school is much different. But that is mistake too. Ms. Cowley mean American system only.

For her most strangest assignment, she make us write about the techniques we use to write a paper for another class. Yes, its true, she assign us to write a paper about writing a paper. Well, what can

I do, most of my classes are either math or science, and we dont have papers. Finally I make up this fake paper in an Asian History course that I never take, just to have something to write. Ms. Cowley like that paper best of all, but I fail it too. I fail all the papers, so no surprise when I fail the final.

Ms. Cowley was impatient person, but in one way she was always patient. Whenever somebody in class mispronounce something, Ms. Cowley use all the time she need to make the student say it right.

One day she did it to a Cambodian guy—make him correct his mispronouncement of a whole sentence. Boo is shy person, ashame of his bad accent, and he suffer much in English. He never speak a word unless Ms. Cowley force him to read, then he bend his face down on his desk and mumble in tiny voice.

Speak up, Boo, Ms. Cowley say, we cant hear you.

But Boo just cant say that sentence right. Ms. Cowley force him to repeat it until his face is hot and his voice is shaking like a leaf. Is he scare, I wonder, or is he mad?

Then he answer my question, because he scream so loud he make us all jump—something like "The typical American youth spend 34 hours per week mezmerize to TV, learning violent attitudes while his muscles turn to flap!" Such a big noise from a little guy. And, funny thing, when he yell like that, he almost say the sentence right.

Boo pick up his books and leave. After, he never return to class. I see him in calculus, so I know he finish that semester, but I hear from a classmate that he leave school. I think Ms. Cowley was his second chance in 002. To me its very sad, because Boo is good in math.

Many times I think about those three students who pass our class. Are they the girls Ms. Cowley like to pet? Also I wander, will more of us pass Mr. Goddard's 002? He seem like more organized teacher and his essay topics are understandable. But he never tell us correct answer to essay question, never even hint us. Usually I don't know what does he want me to write.

When I come home today, I find Rayneece in her room, the door is shut, she is playing her tapes and crying. She cry so loud I can hear even with the music. Whats going on I wander, because she never did this before.

Did she break up with her boyfriend?

*10/6/85*

Stopped by the branch library this evening for some information on Ambrose Bierce. The name keeps coming up in my research. I've been meaning to check him out.

All they had was Bierce's *The Devil's Dictionary*, a hundred pages of word definitions couched in the author's highly condensed ironic style. A few Biercisms:

*Aborigines*, n. Persons of little worth found cumbering the soil of a newly discovered country. They soon cease to cumber; they fertilize.

*Distance*, n. The only thing that the rich are willing for the poor to call theirs and keep.

*Labor*, n. One of the processes by which A acquires property for B.

*Marriage*, n. The state or condition of a community consisting of a master, a mistress and two slaves, making in all, two.

*Reverence*, n. The spiritual attitude of a man to a god and a dog to a man.

I especially like that last. The more I consider it, the truer it seems. What an incisive wit. Reminds me of Donne in its precision, but more bitter than Donne, more edge on the razor.

Bierce is worth looking into. According to the *Dictionary* preface, he wrote stories about the Civil War. Got to see those. A good biography too if I can find one. Check stacks at school.

*Thursday, October 10*

Mr. Goddard give back our narrative paper today. This time I receive CR+ grade (credit plus), very highest one! Teacher write nice comments, including: Please see me if you would be interested in publishing this.

Is he serious? I wander. Publish my paper for 002 class? Dont sound right to me, but I'm curious, so I stay to ask.

I watch his eyes while he talk to me, to see if he's lying or playing a trick. I cant tell, he's a pretty smart guy. When I laugh at his idea to publish my paper, he dont get mad. He just try to convince me. He tell me if I revise the paper good enough, he think some magazine will print it as short story.

"What magazine?" I ask.

He say we will send it to several probably. If I want.

Even though my teacher might be sincere, his high hope to publish my paper seems quite unlikely to me. But, in the other hand, I am so happy with my good grade! And since we are assign to revise at least one essay this semester, I think I am wise to choose this one. When I finish it, if Mr. Goddard still think its good enough to publish, surely he will want me to pass his class. Then only the final exam can stop me.


*10/12/85*

There's a whole shelf of Bierce books in the stacks at school. For starters, I took the most recent biography and a collection of short stories. Also, volume I of *Collected Works*.

*Collected Works* caught my eye because it contains the author's autobiographical prose concerning his Civil War combat. He was in on some of the big ones: Shiloh, Chickamauga, Kinnesaw Mountain (where he suffered a near-fatal head wound). I must say the guy writes well of war. As well as Tolstoy or Hemingway.

His description of Shiloh makes Bosch's Hell look tame. As a greenie, Bierce was among the troops sent to reinforce the depleted Union armies which by end of the first day of fighting had been pinned against the Tennessee River—ripe to be butchered come dawn. All night long the Union boats crossed and recrossed the Tennessee—desperately ferrying over fresh troops, bringing back the wounded.

As Bierce's boat neared shore, deserting Union soldiers, wild-eyed and bedraggled, tried to climb aboard. These men, he explains, had been broken in mind and spirit by the horrific blood-letting of day one. In their stampede to flee they clawed for space needed to transport the injured. This enraged the troops on the boats, who bayoneted them, clubbed them, kicked them back into the river. Bierce saw scores drown. With every arriving boat, the process was repeated.

At one point Bierce calls the deserters a "demented crew of cowards." Their behavior is strange—the antithesis of what one would expect of the military. Poor training would likely be part of the explanation. Early in the Civil War anyone with money was allowed to equip, train, and even lead volunteer regiments into battle. Troops of that kind might well lose discipline the first time they fought.

I believe there was another reason. Combat in those days was brutal. The accepted mode of attack was for successive lines of men to march or run directly into defended positions. They were met by withering musket fire from high caliber, low velocity weapons which did awful damage to the human body. Bierce refers sometimes to the "deadline," that narrow zone just within miniball range where advancing troops turned from heroes into dying meat, falling on those who had fallen before in a long pile of bleeding bodies.

What modern soldier could be sure he packs the heavy-duty balls required to walk into that meat chopper? And the Civil War soldier had to think about it before he did it, sometimes for hours. Much contemporary warfare is kinder in that regard. It happens so fast there is no specific anticipation (though much generalized dread).

For the modern soldier, I would say, the hell is more in reflection. Rambo has the rest of his life to ruminate the almost involuntary braveries and goofs of a few seconds.


*Sunday, October 13*
I was right. Rayneece broke up with her boyfriend. However, she didnt cry for long. She defeat her heartbreak the easy way by find herself a new man. This one is blond, blue eyes. I dont know his name.

Partly, he is cause of fight I have with her last night.

Just before he come to pick her up, Im cooking my dinner, like always, and Rayneece say, cant you do that later? Your making the apartment smell. Whats my friend going to think?

I tell her if she can invite her friend without ask me, then I can cook my food without her permission.

What? she say. Talk so I can understand you girl.

I repeat, try to stay calm.

But she's not even listening. What makes that stink? she ask.

Nothing, I say.

Something does, she say, looking at my food.

I tell her maybe she don't like the fish sauce. Many Americans dont like that smell.

Fish what? she ask.

I show her.

You keep it, she say, pushing my hand. If you want to eat that crap, move back to Japan.

Im not from Japan, I say.

China, whatever.

By now, I'm so mad I want to hit her with fish sauce. I tell her I'm from Vietnam.

No you ain't.

How you know?

Your too tall, she say, like she very wise.

Such ignorance! I inform her people from my country come in all sizes and levels of intelligence, just like Americans.

She look at me, frowning like she want to say something, then go into bathroom, makeup her face, spray her hair.

Later, her boyfriend arrive and they leave.

Now I feel sad. What did our fight prove? Just that we cant get along. Before I move in here, I have this silly idea that me and my roommate will cooperate. For example, we can fix meals together and share food. She can show me American meals I dont know, and I show her Vietnamese dishes she might like. Maybe some nights she will do it all, some nights I do it all, give each other a break, maybe even a surprise. Well, those are the dumb ideas I have in my dreamy head before I learn the true character of my room-mate.

Usually Rayneece don't even bother to fix a meal, she gobble snacks. She love potato chip, pork rines, ding dongs, ice cream. One time I see her eat this big box of marshmellow ice cream with a spoon while she watch TV, she finish it all. I couldnt believe. You cant teach somebody like that to eat a healthy fish for dinner.

I dont know how she keep her nice figure.

*10/15/85*

Been reading the Bierce bio for the past couple days. Rather amaz-ing, but this poor sucker, when he packed off to war, was even more of a Corporal Ernest Candide than Corporal Ernest Candide.

He came from a strongly abolitionist family. His uncle, whom young Bierce much admired, armed John Brown and his boys for their assault on Harper's Ferry. Four days after Lincoln's call for volunteers, Ambrose Bierce (age 18) enlisted—hot to trot with Ser-geant Death.

Even as a disillusioned adult Bierce remained proud of the no-ble purpose that fueled his enlistment. Yet it was the war that disil-lusioned him. The bullet in the skull. Seeing the death and suffering of others. And more even than those, the politicking generals and the needless slaughters they precipitated in their greed, vainglory, and, sometimes, cowardice. As an orderly he saw it all. By war's end he had far greater love for the enemy than for most of the Union generals.

Corporal Ernest Candide experienced the disillusionment en-gendered by war on a more personal level. Initially, in his own mind, he was going to be a heroic angel of the battlefield. His job as combat medic would be to save lives while taking none. He even recorded some such categorical imperative in his journal. During his first five months in country, the corporal carried no weapon more deadly than a syringe. He was able to observe his defining principle with absolute precision.

Then came the morning he found himself pinned down with a badly wounded soldier. Twice Candide got the plasma drip hooked up, and both times a trigger-happy Chuck (holed up in a bunker he'd captured) pegged the suspended plasma bag. The bullet ripped the system out of the soldier's arm, threw it off into the dirt, out of reach. Maddening. The wounded was fast bleeding out from a severed artery too high in his leg for a good tourniquet.

Candide figured he didn't really have a choice. He took a grenade from the belt of the wounded, pulled the pin, waited till he thought Charlie was reloading, then charged the bunker and delivered through the slit. As he dove for dirt the bunker blew fire and concussion ripped at his eardrums.

Later, when the area was secure and the casualties had been lifted out—including the soldier with the torn artery, still alive—Corporal Candide went to see what was in the bunker. It was a teenager, like himself, a skinny one, sitting up against the wall, dead, in a pool of blood. He'd lost a forearm and was torn open below the ribcage. He must have picked up the grenade just before it blew.

The corporal was forced to revise his categorical imperative. "Thou shalt not kill" became "Thou shalt not kill unless to save life." He began carrying a .45, which encumbered him only slightly in his medical work.

Not long after, Candide's squad, walking an enemy supply trail, surprised fifteen VC grubbing down. There were only five GIs. When several of the enemy went for their weapons, Candide knew he had to act.

Even amidst the split-second confusion the distinctive work of the .45 was all too obvious. It was dismaying, sickening business. Fish in a barrel. That was the feeling. Fortunately, four of them surrendered by throwing themselves face down with their arms over their heads. Those we took captive. Of the 11 we killed, three were definitely mine.

That evening the chagrined corporal abandoned categorical imperatives, having lost faith in their utility. The most important of the ideals he'd brought with him to war had been razed by his own hand. He'd replaced them with nothing but bitter knowledge and a perturbing question: What might he be willing to do to preserve his precious hide?

*Wednesday, October 16*

Rayneece new friend is Kevin. He's not so bad, by himself. I talk to him for some minutes when Rayneece is in shower. He is USC student. He wanted to be dentist, but now his grades are too low to get in dentist school, so he try to decide new major.

He mention he is Teek. Im not sure what it is, so I smile like it is a good thing. He seem proud. Is Teek his culture group? He looks like some ordinary white guy.

My calculus test today was hard, harder than I expect. Maybe I did okay, but I worry. I feel sleepy during whole exam and it seem like my brain go slow. I did not finish two problem, not good.

The reason I am sleepy is because Rayneece and Kevin been keep me awake. Every night at 1:00 am or 2:00 they come home, drink beer in living room, talk loud, play TV. Then they go in her room, close door, and you know what. I think Rayneece is uncapable to do it quietly.

*10/17/85*

Staff meeting this afternoon, at which the Humper triumphantly announced the findings of her frigging survey: most of our basic writing students are illiterate in their first languages, therefore probably can't be expected to learn English or any other language. They are near-incurable linguistic dunces, verbal retards.

Subtext (as I see it): our students' imbecility explains why so many of them fail the composition finals. It also justifies the finals as a ruthless weeding mechanism. If our students don't have a real language to contain learning, then all the knowledge we pour into them will fly out like water through a sieve. So college is a waste.

In the Humper's finest hour as scientific researcher, one sour note was sounded. But no one took it seriously I should think. The oaf pointed out naively that our retarded students all passed the verbal portion of their SATs. Those needing it also passed the TOEFL test, certifying their university-level command of English. How were those successful test scores possible given our students' stunted verbal abilities?

More Humping Power's regal silence announced the advent of toady time.

Ann Cowley went first in her whiny voice. "John, a student came to me recently, a Cambodian girl who failed my 001 class last spring. Now she's failing her second try, with another teacher, and she wondered if I had advice. As we talked, I learned she'd missed four years of school in Cambodia because of the holocaust. Then the poor thing said, 'Ms. Cowley, How can I learn to write English good when I don't even know Cambodian?'"

Ann smiled patiently and continued. "So many students tell similar stories. What Mary is saying coincides with what all of us see in class, I think. Is it right to squander taxpayer money on students who lack the basic tools to learn?" She looked around the table for agreement.

Chris Seifert, as usual, provided some. "Seems to me Mary's made an honest attempt to determine why so many of our students fail." He caught my eye. "John, the purpose of the national exams is to establish who *enters* college. But if they come here and can't cut it, it's cruel to pretend they can. I'm not saying we shouldn't help them, either. Maybe we could set up special programs. Language programs. Or vocational schools, where they could be taught job skills not requiring language."

"Job skills not requiring language? Train them to be seeing-eye dogs, you mean, or pack mules?"

A few snickers erupted involuntarily, stifled immediately by MHP's searchlight eyes. "Since our discussion seems to be descending to the ridiculous," she said, "let's move along."

As we moved along, I looked around the table at all my fellow part-time writing instructors (our powerless majority). I saw again what I had seen before—a mostly talented and dedicated crew, but sullen and fatigued, stretched thin by too many years of too many classes on too many campuses at too little pay. Vastly lacking in job security anywhere. They know MHP's study is bogus, her stats probably fabricated, but are afraid to speak up for fear of losing classes next semester. Only because I happen to have specialized training and some publications can I run my mouth a little more without repercussions (so far).

During the rest of the meeting MHP ignored me whenever I raised my hand. When I tried to edge my voice in, her toadies talked over me. In short, business as usual.


*Friday, October 18*

Since I pick my narrative essay as my paper to revise, I rewrite it three times, make it good as I can. However, I feel it must have grammars in it, perhaps many. So I go to Writing Center yesterday for help.

The tutor they assign me is American, name Karen. She is some few years older than me. A kindly person, I believe, and good at her job. First she explain comma splicers and we find all the ones in my paper. Then I fix. Second, she show me how to put in those little commas that go up high, like when you write Becky's dog. Last, she say my verb tenses need work, but since we don't have time for it I will return next week. Oh yes, she show me quote marks too.

Maybe my narrative is better than I think. When Karen finish reading it first time, I see tear on her eye. Also, she give me high compliments, like my teacher. Maybe Mr. Goddard was telling the truth.


*10/20/85*

Played basketball this afternoon for the first time since the sprain. The ankle's still a little stiff, but it held up. It was the rest of me that crapped.

I knew I was in poor shape so I went to Maravilla Park early in the morning, hoping to avoid a game. I hadn't been there ten minutes when three kids in their late teens showed up and talked me into two on two.

Those little twerps flat ran me into the court. First, my wind went. Next my legs cashed in. After that I missed all my shots while the guy I was guarding rained in fade aways from all over the court. I just couldn't move my lead legs fast enough to cover him.

Me and my partner got whacked 15-6, something like that.

Wheezing and sweating profusely, I begged off seconds, staggered to a grassy plot under a tree and collapsed. One of the cardplayers on the bench beside me looked me over and shook his grizzled head. "Take a rain check, man. Ain't worth it."

He's right. The ball courts on this end of town are no scene for the out-of-shape geezer, even on a slow morning. I need to rebuild my wind before I try that shit again.

*Sunday, October 20*

Last night Kevin bring a friend name Neal, a tall guy who smile all the time even when nothing is funny. Rayneece stay up with them till after 4:00 am, play music, drink beer, talk and laugh.

This morning when I go to fix something to eat, I find Neal snoring on the livingroom couch. Then I see the beer can next to him. It is fall over, all the beer is leak on carpet, make big dark spot and stink.

I fill a pan with hot water and cleaner, try to scrub the beer away. The noise wakes Neal. He moan. "Can't you do that somewhere else?"

"This is where you spill the beer," I say. "If you spill in kitchen, I clean there."

Why are American kids more immature than kids in Vietnam, I wander. Then I remember I was quite childish sometimes when I was there. My brother too. I also remember other Vietnamese kids who were immature. Dao, my brother's friend, was a sweet person, but she expect to get her way every time, and if she don't her whole face suck up in a pout.

It's easy for anyone to be immature if your parents protect you from life, and if they have money to spoil you. My father, and even more my grandfather, often treat me like baby and give me all the presents I want. Maybe, if I live like that till now, never suffer at all, never lose anything important, then I will be like Rayneece and her friends—still somewhat childish at adult age.

But I don't believe I will get drunk, even if I am completely spoil. I don't know why they do it. Can't they see it's going to make you feel awful the next day?

*10/22/85*

Running's the obvious way for me to get back in shape, but I've resisted it because I have such a wretched picture of your typical Southern California sidewalk squirrel. He (sometimes she) is a precious arrogance on the move, comic in posture, fully accessorized with sun visor, garish shades, Sony headset, plastic water bottle, fluttering pastel skivvies, and high-tech running shoes modeled rather obviously on the formula one race car.

I mean consider it. For two million years mankind runs in bare feet and a loincloth—or less. Now, in just one lame-brained century, probably as a result of breathing too much smog, we've achieved the super absurdity of the modern jogger. Are we leaving sufficient scope for future human runners to make even greater fools of themselves? It worries me.

Still, I decided to give it a try. No way to build the wind quicker so far as I know, and, unlike ball, I can choose my own decrepit pace. I'm putting it to myself like this. My sort of jogging is military style, as in Army basic, a no-nonsense quest with the cinders.

This afternoon I walked up to school in my sweats and sneakers, did some stretching exercises on the infield, then cruised the track with a stiff wind popping the stadium flags. Beautiful day. Blue blue sky and radiant sun. Had the whole place to myself.

In the backstretch, with the wind behind me, I built speed to a 90% sprint and held it for a hundred yards or so, body gliding, blood pumping, legs stretching to grab the track. Mind repeating the old mantra—relax relax relax. Such a fine feeling. Always love it. My main connection to sport.

Later I tried a pace I could sustain. Did a mile that way, walked two laps, ran another mile. Followed with windsprints on the infield, pushups, situps. Cooled off by walking home.

Got an excellent workout. My body is heavy and stiff tonight, but also serene, fulfilled, happy. Just might get some real sleep.

*Thursday, October 24*

Yesterday Karen helped me fix verb errors in my narrative essay. It took the whole conference because there are so many. That was kind of discouraging, and it's more discouraging what she tell me. She say I will make mistakes in English verbs for a long time. It's because Vietnamese verbs are so different. If I want to learn faster, I must read books in English, speak English with Americans. But even if I do these, it will take some years before I can use verbs like an American.

I find out Mr. Goddard did not mark all the verb errors in my paper—not even half! Ms. Cowley hardly mark our grammars at all, because she's lazy. In other ways, as I know, Mr. Goddard is not lazy. He write many comments on my papers, and I see he do it for other students too. No, he's not lazy—but why can't he mark all my verb grammars? Don't I need to see my mistakes so I can improve?

Last night I write my story again, try to be perfect, maybe make zero mistake. After class, I give it to my teacher.

He notice there is no title.

"Oh." I didn't consider that.

He say the title usually hint what the story is about.

"Death," I say, but that sound stupid. I tell him forget it.

"Minh and Dao?" he ask.

Sounds good to me. I write it on top of my paper.

I am so glad it's finish, it is too much work.

*10/25/85*

Graded papers all day to clear Saturday and Sunday for work on the novel. Such was my grading frenzy I didn't remember until I was eating dinner that today's my fucking birthday.

The birthday boy.

Well, missed it again. No chocolate cake or blazing candles. No champagne corks ricocheting off the chandelier.

This is, I calculate, the 18th birthday in a row I've *not* celebrated. I'm waiting for the year when I sail right through it, oblivious to the new notch on my gravestone until days, maybe weeks later. At that point, I'll truly be free of the idiocy of birthdays.

*Saturday, October 26*

The new paper for my English class is concern with lying. I must tell my opinion on when lies are okay, and when they are wrong.

I find that this subject is rather complex. I do tell lies some time, and I think maybe a few are okay, like when I tell someone they look good when they look ugly, because I know truth will hurt. But, in the other hand, I regret some lies so deeply.

The biggest lie I ever make in my life was the one I use to trick the Coberlys to become my sponsor. Back then, I live in refugee camp in Tennessee. One day I went to camp office with another Vietnamese girl, a friend of mine sort of, Sylvia La, and we both apply for sponsors. On the application, where it ask for religion, I start to write Buddhist but Sylvia stop me. "Write Catholic," she say, "or you'll never get a sponsor."

She scare me enough that I do it. She also talk me into change my name. Instead of Tien, I write Tina on that form, then later I must repeat it on other forms they give me. Because of that, Tina become my official name.

Anyway, after I lie on my application, and the Coberlys agree to sponsor me, then I have to pretend to them that I am Catholic girl every day, because the Coberlys are very religious. Often I must watch them and imitate their actions, in order to appear Catholic. I make mistakes, but always I explain, "That's how we do in Vietnam."

In my closet, I keep my Buddist shrine on a tray, and when the Coberlys go to bed, I bring it out. The tray contain a small Buddha statue, pictures of my family members, a brass elephant full of little holes to hold my incense.

One day while I'm at school, Mrs. Coberly clean my closet, find the tray. She and her husband are very worry for my soul and when I get home they ask me many questions. I tell them in my land Catholics are allow to honor the family ancestors, such as I do, and even Buddha if we want. But Mr. Coberly say it's wrong, he's certain. He say I am making sacrifice to a graven image, which it is big sin for the Catholics.

The Coberlys let me keep the photos of my family, but they make me throw Lord Buddha in the trash. I feel bad about that, because it shows terrible disrespect, but I tell myself it is only a statue.

Kindly, the Coberlys give me big crucifix of poor Jesus dying on the cross. Mr. Coberly nail him on the wall over my bed, it's quite scary to look up in the dark and see him there. Often, he keep me awake, because I feel he stare at me. He stare at me because I am liar.

Well, I deserve it. It was a selfish lie, quite unfair to the Coberlys. There are many Catholics among my people, and the Coberlys could of found one to live with them. Better for all of them, better for me too maybe.

Yesterday, Dr. Kim return our calculus tests. I receive 93, A–, third best in class. I'm happy, because I thought I did bad on that test. Lucky for me Dr. Kim give partial credit on the problems I can't finish.


*10/27/85*

Been running most every day. Evenings seem to work best right now. The past couple of days have been hot, over 90, but as the sun goes down a breeze develops off the ocean, cooling the air to about 65 by nightfall.

Running is easy and pleasant then and the city is in a way beautiful, with the sky changing color from oranges and reds to the deeper bruise colors, purple and black. As heaven loses light, the city core highrises brighten to become, together, the glowingest mass around, dwarfing the moon. Out of downtown crawl six lanes of densely packed headlamps—a long shimmering glacier of light. Into the gloom under the temples of Mammon fly six lanes of well-spaced red taillights.

Ran two miles tonight at moderate pace. Making progress, but I'll never be a distance runner. Not built for it. I've also put too much smoke through the old lungs.

*Tuesday, October 29*

As I study for midterms in Physics and Symbolic Logic, Rayneece provide entertainment with her boyfriend situation.

This afternoon when I come home from school her door is close, but I hear voices—and one is a guy. So I think, it's Kevin in there, who else?

Neal come out, take my glass from kitchen cabinet, drink water at sink. He is barefoot, no shirt, sweaty all over, hair stick up in back. After three glasses he burp, smile big smile at me.

"Neal, could you bring me a coke?" Rayneece ask. She is in bed, under covers.

Neal takes her the coke. Then he gets dress, leave.

Rayneece shower, make up her face. Before she finish there is knock on door. It's Kevin. I go in my room, but I can hear them talking. Kevin ask Rayneece if she see Neal.

"No," she say. "Why?"

"He ditched intermural practice."

"Why would I see him?"

"I don't know."

Sounds like Rayneece is going to learn a lesson. Kevin is suspicious, I think.

Maybe I can use her in my English paper about lying.


*10/29/85*

Linda called tonight. Talk about voices from the past. It's been what—six years? Seven, I guess. Haven't heard from her since the week after I left.

She called from Missouri, where she lives on a farm with a husband and three rugrats. Does she still paint? Yes, she still paints. Sounds like she's beginning to make the scene there in the Midwest. Between milking cows and gathering eggs, I take it. Mama's got blue sky above, Ozarks all around, and a loving understanding papa who plays alto sax at a club in KC.

Well, I had to hand it to her. It's everything she always wanted. And she deserves it. Fine woman there. I congratulated her.

She asked what I was up to. As I filled her in, the conversation turned on me, her voice taking an edge. "The life you describe sounds lonely, John. You're still pushing people away, aren't you?"

"You know me."

"Think you can make yourself happy that way?"

I was out of patience. "It's as good as marrying some hornboy on the rebound."

"You, buster, are going to be one very sad old misanthrope when you grow up. I feel sorry for you."

And she hung up.

Much residual bitterness there, obviously. Suppose I deserve it. However difficult for me at the time, I should have taken the trouble to help her see why I had to leave, and that it had nothing to do with her. I mean I did explain it, but not in a way she could understand. She still thinks I did it to hurt her, or because of her.

As to me becoming a sad old misanthrope—fat fucking chance. Won't be alive that long.


*Thursday, October 31*

Tonight Rayneece go with Kevin to Halloween party at Teeks, which is fraternity I learn. Kevin dress as vampire, and Rayneece, I dont know what she dress as, but she wear a tiny skirt, sexy stockings, lots of makeup. To me she look like prostitute.

I think I might like a costume party. It could be fun to dress like somebody else and pretend to be that person. It is boring to be yourself always. Especially if you are a somewhat boring person.

In Vietnam, our big holiday in fall season is Festival of the Moon. It happen on the night the moon is biggest and brightest of all the year. Crowds of people walk on the streets and kids carry paper lanterns shape like rabbits, dragons, other animals. Each lantern hang from stick on a string, and one candle burn inside. The kids like to swing the lanterns, make light drawings in the dark.

Always my father take our family to the river on that night. He buy us moon cakes and candies, we sit on the grass by the water, watch the boats pass. The boats are full of people and cover with lanterns of many color. Everyone waits for the moon to rise.

When it comes, it is huge and orange, fat in the middle like Buddha. As it rise higher, it turns white and not quite as big, but still big. It is so bright it hurts your eyes. You can see every bump and hole on the moon's face, seem like you can reach out and touch it almost.

When I was small girl, I think if I stand on my father's shoulders, reach my arm up in the sky, I can touch it. So my father let me try. I find the moon is a little too far away.

10/31/86

Why is it Halloween gets bigger every year? On campus today as the afternoon wore on I saw increasing numbers of warlocks and ghouls, two in my last class. This evening as I walked to the track goblins and hobgoblins of all sizes and every wart teemed on the streets. Some were trick-or-treaters, but as many were adults on their way to parties. It's like the whole city's haunted.

Seems to me all the American holidays are undergoing metamorphosis to versions of themselves more in keeping with our upscale, heady times. Halloween (once a harvest festival) has become in our day an urban saturnalia, a candy glut for the kids and drunken mating rite for adults. Generously, we've invited back as honored Halloween guests all the witches and devils our ancestors burned out of existence in the early days of our Christian republic.

The Americanized Christmas trumpets Jehovah's marriage with Capitalism by commemorating the birth of bouncing baby Mammon. It is a hectic, cutthroat and inebriated season, measured in inventory flux and punctuated by the annual yuletide spike on the Census Bureau's suicide graph.

Easter Sunday is the living dream of kiddie heaven-on-earth, with frolics in Elysian fields courtesy of Walt Disney and his corporate dwarves. It's the holiday simply too precious for words, with happy hopping bunnies, cute candy critters, and nuggets of pastel cholesterol lurking in the bluegrass. More children chuck up on Easter than on any other holiday (except Halloween).

Then there's Memorial Day, with it's festive first stoking of the summer barbecues. Here the underlying theme is human sacrifice by auto crash, as thundering engines and screaming gears at Indianapolis are echoed a millionfold on the nation's highways, racking up a death toll carefully monitored by the media and reported every hour. Down the years, the main sentiment behind this holiday has changed little: What's good for General Motors is good for the USA.

And let us not omit the 4th of July (formerly Independence Day), our enthusiastic national tip of the hat to enfeeblement by the life of Riley. This jubilee's contemporary spirit is best depicted by a smog-gray flag studded with crushed beer cans and, in the center, a T-bone steak over crossed waterskis. It's the one day of the year on which that rapid-fire popping up the street might be a harmless string of firecrackers.

Blessed be our land for its many gleeful days of celebration.


*Tuesday, November 5*
Last night, after my other homeworks, I write my essay on lying for English. I find it confusing and hard. I stay up late, start over many times. Finally I finish, but it's weak I think.

After my classes today I am very tire. I call Robert, tell him I'm sick and can't come in. Then I fall asleep on my bed.

I wake in late afternoon. There is loud argument. Two guys are yelling at each other just outside my door. Then I hear them fighting. They push over chairs, knock the kitchen table into wall, crash against my door. Finally they stop.

The front door slam and through window I see Kevin walk fast on lawn. He jump in his car, spin his tires on street and speed away, almost hit another car.

I open my door and see Neal sitting at kitchen table, bleeding his nose on paper towel. He looks angry. There is red mark on his forehead. Rayneece is in the living room picking up her broken lamp. I find two of my cactus plants crush, have to throw away. Fortunately, that's all the damage.

Now I learn Neal will stay here tonight. Maybe he can't go back to the Teeks. I hope he doesn't want to live here.

*11/6/85*

Read most of the Bierce biography yesterday. What a fascinating, screwed-up guy. He was a war hero, literary lion, the most powerful political journalist of his era, but endured a private life riddled with tragedy.

Sadly, the persons who most loved and admired this charming, irascible, and brutally honest egoist profited least from their relationships with him. Bierce's older son, Day, following in the footsteps of the dad he idolized, ran away from home as a teenager to become a boozing, brawling frontier journalist. Young Bierce though lacked his pop's steely gravitas—required to pull off such a preposterous macho masquerade. Within months of leaving home, in a drunken rage over being jilted and with the weapon favored by his dad (a .45 revolver), Day gunned down his best friend and tried to kill his girlfriend too, before blowing himself away.

Leigh, Bierce's younger son, lacked the violent temperament of his father and brother, but was their equal in heroic escapades with a bottle. In the family tradition, he too ran away from home in his teens to become a journalist. He succeeded for a time, at both gathering the news and drinking, but then got plastered on the job one winter night in New York City and lay down on the sidewalk to snooze with a snowbank for pillow. The atrocious cold he caught steadily worsened in ensuing weeks until it drove his coffin nails. Falling asleep outdoors at night while wasted happened to be another family tradition.

Molly, Bierce's wife, seems to have loved her husband deeply all her adult life. However, at one point fairly early in their unhappy union, perhaps provoked by Ambrose's long absences and frequent infidelities, Mrs. Bierce made the fatal error of permitting an admirer to send her two love letters, which she never answered but kept. Bierce found the letters and, it appears, the mortal shock to his gargantuan self-esteem propelled him to separate from his wife forever. He refused to even speak to her again, though he always sent money for her support. Apparently he was able to convince her that her punishments were deserved.

When she was in her sixties, rumors reached Molly that her husband had found a young charmer he wanted to marry. Mrs. Bierce began divorce proceedings, to generously give her man his freedom, but had a heart attack in the process, freeing him that way. Many thought she died of emotional trauma. The new marriage, by the way, never happened.

Bierce's war buddies, his protegés, his old flames, and his favorite brother Albert all became targets for his ire as he got older. In the author's last years he broke off with nearly all of them and began to taunt the few who still kept in touch by conveying to them his developing plans to join the Mexican Revolution, on foot or on horseback, as a severely asthmatic septuagenarian.

Then he actually did it, vanishing into the Mexican desert. Not long after his brother Albert died of apoplexy.

It would seem Bierce's personal attractiveness was a death trap. The violence deep in his being, planted by genetics perhaps, and amplified by his war experiences, powered the productive ambitions of this strong soul. But somehow that same violent streak also infected and destroyed those weaker souls who loved him. At least that's how it looks to me.

He should have known better than to get involved with people. He was lonely, as all of us are, but failed to see that he needed to protect others from too-close contact with himself. Had he consistently chosen isolation, he might have stood at the vortex of only one tragedy: his own. But he was a little too selfish.


*Friday, November 8*
In English class yesterday we debate where is better to live, city or country?

I choose the city, because I'm thinking I am city girl. However, as we debate, so many arguments on the other side sound good to me. For instance, in the rural area there is not much crime. Life in the country is less competitive and people are more friendly. Plus, man and nature live in better harmony in the country. All these seem true to me.

Then I realize I am not really a city girl. Can Tho, where I grow up, is quite different from a big city like Saigon or Los Angeles. Can Tho is more like a town. Life there is slow and easy. Some streets are busy, but the air is clean and at night you can see the stars.

My favorite place of all is in the country just outside Can Tho—my grandfather's farm. It is the farm where my ancestors live for many generations, and where my grandparents retire after they give the business to my dad. I use to visit them often, much more than my brother, who never want to leave his friends.

My grandparents were very free with me, especially for a girl. At age nine, they let me explore the farm and the rice fields by myself. Granddad would rent out the paddies to poor farmers, and sometimes I play with the farmers' kids, when they dont have work. We go down to the river, throw sticks and rocks in the water. But we can't swim because it's too strong and deep.

Sometimes Grandfather take me fishing on the river, which he like to do. I did not like fishing much, because I did not like to hook the fishes. Grandfather tell me the fishes can't feel the hook, but this I never believe. I think its just a lie people tell to make fisherman feel better.

I did like to sit beside river and watch the birds fly over the water, or a snake swimming, or else lay back in the grass and look at the clouds. Later I like fishing too, after Grandfather let me fish without a hook. I never catch anything but so what?

He teach me religion too. My parents were not very religious, and certainly not my brother, so Grandfather decide he must train me, even though I am a girl. He feel I have a strong spiritual nature like him.

He explain what the Buddha teach: to lead good life, don't be selfish, don't hurt other people or animals either, and always be kind to the weak and misfortunate.

He also instruct me in proper way to honor our ancestors who live as spirits in the family shrine. He show how to make gifts with fruit and other food, how to burn money and say prayers, how to clean shrine without disturbing its sensitive guests.

"If we care for our ancestors in the proper way," he tell me, "give them a good home and our love, they will bring prosperity to the house, and when evil comes they will warn us in dreams."

"But if we neglect the shrine, forget to do the rituals, let dust collect, our disrespect will drive our ancestors out into the world. They will wander without a home, weaklings in the kingdom of the dead, at the mercy of anything."

Grandfather also say, when the spirits leave a family, the people in the family have no guide after that. "They are like babies in the jungle." He used to scare me with that stuff when I was little girl. Later, when I was a teenager, I begin to doubt. I think maybe it's all just superstition, like so many foolish things people believe.

When the communist put my grandfather in re-education camp to teach him how to think like Uncle Ho, all my family ignore the shrine, the offerings, the prayers, including me. And in the time that follow, look what happen to us: the family is destroy. It turn out exactly like Grandfather say.

So I will keep a shrine always, it is a place where the spirits of my family can be happy and live in peace. And I feel more secure with them near me. My family's spirits have been with me for more than three years—all except my brother. His ghost is still lost, I believe, and so I worry. Some ghosts never find there way home and they suffer a lot.


*11/10/85*

I'm getting to know some of the track regulars who run in the evening. Most of them I like, though we never speak. My feeling is we're engaged in this mutual healthy endeavor under the stars.

One woman I see frequently is Chinese I think, in her forties and seriously overweight. She jogs at a slow pace (slower than I walk) always in the far outside lane. She clocks many laps that way, steady as a metronome.

Two Chicanas in their thirties often jog together at a moderate pace in the middle lanes. One is getting back in shape, the other maintaining that which cannot be improved.

Then there's the professor—middle-aged, balding, with thick gray beard, pudgy middle, and legs like hickory sticks. From those legs I'd guess he's been running for years.

The boxer is a mystery, his angular face lost in shadow inside the loose sweathood. He runs doggedly, with stubby strides, not on the track but on the infield grass next to the curb, where he's worn a groove.

Since we're talking Los Angeles, you also have your smattering of track squirrels. These are male and better than average runners, but jerks. They seem to feel they own the track by virtue of their skills and are of the attitude that when they come tooling by, all duds should butt out and watch from the sidelines with awe and applause.

One of these motating dung heaps found himself a nasty little trick. In passing, he'll speed up and come as close as possible, maybe clip you, trying to spook. Anyone is fair game, women and the elderly included. I've seen him make runners stumble or step over the curb in surprise. No doubt this gives him a thrill.

Tonight when he brushed my arm I was ready with a trick of my own, one I learned as a receiver. I accelerated to match strides, meshed my legs with his, and gunned it. He went down hard behind me, asshole over elbows. Heard him grunt as he landed.

I thought he might wait till I circled the track, perhaps take issue over his little contretemps, but apparently the fall dampened his spirits. I watched from the backstretch as he picked himself up and limped off to his car.

Doubt he'll be back. Score one for humanity.


*Monday, November 11*

I did not need to worry about Neal live with us. Rayneece dump him already. If he call, she say "Tell him I'm out." She usually is out—with her new man.

He's older, about 40. He has deep, relax voice, sunglasses and a gold chain on his neck. He say he own some restaurants, but I don't know. To me he is not completely trustable person.

In one way, he seem like good choice. He and Rayneece are same race. That's better because you don't shock society, and also, if you marry, you know what color the babies will be. Plus, people of same race can often understand each other better, which helps make the relationship strong, in my opinion.

I just wish Rayneece could find a *nice* black man. This guy, I don't know.


*11/12/85*
Been thinking about big bro the past couple days. The happiest year of my life was probably the one we played football together.

From the time Gary went out for the team his sophomore year we worked out together religiously five or six days a week. We set up a weight room in the corner of the barn, ran on country roads around the ranch, took all the heavy chores, from stacking hay to pulling rocks to tightening fence. Just ate it up. Gary figured that by doing many different types of training we were developing more muscle groups, for all-around strength and flexibility.

Maybe he was right. I know that by the time I started high school I was ready for football—ready beyond belief. I'd been living it in my head for two years, attending all Gary's games, riding to the away games as a mascot on the team bus. For me, joining my hero on the field of battle was the greatest honor. For him, I don't know. I doubt he thought about it.

I can still see him frozen on the line in front of me during the count, rising with the snap, moving like a plow through the defense, no matter who they were. All season Gary opened big holes for me and I ran through them, setting a conference rushing record as our team went 10-1. We would have been undefeated, but Gary broke his ankle in the first quarter of our final game and had to be pulled. I was held to 43 yards that day, and we lost by 2 points.

Gary was not that big—never more than 215—but he was unusually strong. His secret was conditioning, and a certain methodical ruthlessness. All the time we watched TV at home he'd be squeezing a rubber ball in his right hand to improve his already terrific grip. He used that grip on the tender belly flesh of defensive linemen: to administer extreme pain, pinching and twisting. Lester Philman, Goodland's all-state tackle, at 280 pounds intimidated most everybody in our neck of the woods. But Gary reduced Lester's game to agonized cussing and fear farts. He never got past my brother the whole afternoon.

Despite the diddly size of our school and the relative obscurity of our conference, Gary received many college offers. Folks around Hill City shit a brick when he rejected them all to take a small academic scholarship to Kansas University.

I couldn't believe it either. I was sure he'd blown his mind on acid, which he'd been experimenting with heavily. His piddling scholarship meant he'd have to work part-time, instead of playing football. I asked him why. Was it because he broke his ankle?

He explained that football was a kid's game, not worth serious attention now that he was 18. Time to grow up.

I thought back on all the work we'd done, all the physical and mental devotion we'd lavished on football. I mean I thought we were preparing for college ball, at least, the way we were going after it. Pissed, I asked him what all that was about.

"Fun, Johnny. To have fun."

I was dumbfounded. "Fun?"

"Not enough?"

Sure football was fun, but somehow I'd always assumed there was a larger purpose than fun. And, by the way, weren't there better ways to have fun than by busting your tail, taking cheap shots, and playing welcome mat for oversized bodies? His attitude really jawed me.

In the fall he left for college and a new (adult) life—while I confronted two more years of kid stuff.

Our redoubtable Panthers did well those years. We won the conference both seasons and my senior year we went 11-0. Along the way, I twice more set new conference rushing records. But it wasn't the same. I was functioning on rote, for the team, for the coach, for my parents and friends—simply because I didn't know what else to do.

It wasn't just my brother's decision to quit football either. With his class, many of the best players in our league graduated. The competition fell to a lower level and the glory was gone. I triumphed without much enthusiasm during the Lilliputian Wars, as I saw them.

*Tuesday, November 12*
Today in English we write in-class essay on city vs. country. I did poor, I believe, because I get confuse. For many reasons of my heart I want to live in the country, but the more I consider, my rational intelligence suggest big advantages I find in city.

Isn't it true there are more hospitals and better medical care in the city? Those matter a lot, especially when you get old. Most libraries and colleges are in the city, so you must go there for knowledge. And the city is where are the jobs. If you choose country to live, you must often settle for lesser level career, less money—maybe no job at all.

Finally, I see so many positives and negatives on both sides of this issue that my head ache and my argument go back and forth like a snake. And what is my thesis? I guess it is I want to live in both country and city—all I need is two bodies.

Fortunately, there was some good news. Mr. Goddard hand back our papers on lying and I get CR– on that one. In English, even the lowest passing grade is good enough for me any time. All I want is to pass.

At work Robert give my first job evaluation. He mark me EX-CELLENT in everything except "Takes supervision willingly." For that, he mark FAIR.

I am surprise he grade so high. He didn't have to, because I do make mistakes. Also, these days, I study homeworks on the job almost as much as him.

I think probably he is decent person under his superior act. He only pretends he doesn't care about others.

*11/13/85*

At today's staff meeting, the Hump made manifest what she's been hinting for some time. She wants us *not* to help our students prepare for the final exams. Exams which determine their course grades 100%.

To a lay person, this stance may appear bizarre. But then, the lay person, in the naivety of layhood, will assume that one clear goal of any teacher is to help students find the knowledge they need to pass. How sadly misinformed the laity can be.

The Humper, a seasoned professional in the field of writing instruction, is not deluded by surface appearances. She knows that when teachers help students prepare for the final, something sinister is on the bud—a strain of pedagogical cancer known as "coaching."

Students who are "coached," she explained today, are robbed of the rich intellectual challenge of figuring everything out for themselves. As a result, they lose confidence in their native linguistic abilities and the learning process collapses.

Predictably, the malcontent among us raised his carping voice. "A month ago you proved our students don't have linguistic abilities. How can they lose confidence in what they don't possess?"

Encouraging the wellsprings of democracy, MHP looked around the table for a toady defender, but none was forthcoming (probably out of resentment over her new way of hamstringing our ability to teach).

So she swatted me down herself. "The fact that many of our students test low in linguistic development is the reason for this meeting, John. My point is, we don't help such students by coaching. Coaching puts them on crutches."

Of course, how logical. Little mental crutches. So that's what I've been up to. I'm a damned crutch purveyor.

Just to save time, I gave up protest and let her proceed to analyze the motives of the teacher "coach." Her eyes were on me most of the time. Perhaps she felt I most needed the lesson.

Coaches, we learned, are the pimps of academic failure. These weak-willed bleeding hearts hold aloft to their pupils the false hope of an easy way out. Why? To win a popularity contest, obviously.

There is no easy way out, according to the Humper. Success is never easy. Success is only possible when motivated students are led by an honest noncoaching teacher who provides "a series of challenging, pedogogically sound writing assignments." These assignments "stretch the students' skill levels" so as to raise them to "writing competence" by the end of the semester. Just in time for the final.

Her words fell into such cold silence that even her witch's skin felt it. With no response from any of us, the meeting sped to conclusion.

Later, I reflected on it all. Here is what it seems to boil down to. The Hump wants us to teach like her number one echo, Ann Cowley. Ann has been following the noncoaching plan for three years now—and almost none of her students pass!

MHP's true goal becomes clearer every day. She doesn't merely want hordes of students to fail, she wants them *all* to fail—every single one if possible. Call it the Auschwitz approach to writing instruction. The educational final solution. Of course, as yet, it's only an ideal. Some students still squeak through. But Hump's working on it.


*Thursday, November 14*
Rayneece is gone since Monday night. Then she return this morning with her new boyfriend. She hurry because they have to catch a plane.

As she pack, her friend smoke a cigarette on the couch. To be polite I ask where they are going. Also I am somewhat curious.

He say a place I don't know.

I guess he see ignorance on my face because he repeat, "A-ca-pul-co. You know. South of the boredom." He point to the wall with his thumb and give big smile. It feel strange because I can't see his eyes behind his dark glasses.

Later, when they leave, I look in my atlas. I think I find that place, in Mexico, on the coast. It's about 3000 kilometers away.

What's down there?

*11/15/85*

Gerry Minter came to my office this morning with some friendly advice. Told a touching parable about how he, as a young teacher, had fallen into the seemingly innocent practice of coaching.

Big surprise. Our department chair has joined the pod people. Been bitten by the Humper I guess. I was curious about the depth of his delusion so I asked what was wrong with coaching.

"When you coach, John, you do their thinking for them. At least that's the danger. Personal discovery is the key to cognitive development, not rote. The teacher is only a facilitator, a catalyst. We can open the door, but they must walk through."

I was thinking, here is a brain softened by too many conferences and committee meetings. Before the softening, no great wattage anyway.

I reminded him that most of our students are teenagers, and the majority have been in the U.S. only a few years. How did he expect them to write intelligently about capital punishment or abortion if they'd never really thought about the concepts before, as most hadn't. Abortion may be a white-hot issue in the U.S., but it's a virtual non-issue in most of the countries our students come from. Do the Cambodians, for example, have time to worry about abortion or capital punishment with their government systematically wiping out the adult population?

Gerry felt it was high time for our students to participate fully in the new society they'd adopted. Time to begin dealing with American issues.

Fine, I countered, but how can they learn to deal with American issues if we flunk them out of school? And what's wrong with a teacher helping them understand the issues?

Around and around we went, slowly arriving nowhere. In the end, he was annoyed by my reluctance to see the light. He recrossed his long legs, adjusted his glasses. "I just found that when I coached, all the papers came out sounding the same. They were canned, with no original thought whatsoever. Worse yet, the wrong students tended to pass."

"The wrong students?"

His eyes went cold. "You know who I mean. The lamentable intellects who cling to three basic arguments like driftwood on the high seas and who don't know a comma from an apostrophe. Are we doing such students a favor by pretending they're up to college work?"

Jesus, I was thinking, he's for sure been bitten by the Humper bat. I had to remind myself that his visit was a mission of collegiality, in his own eyes at least. As chair, he could have scheduled our talk for his office and treated me more like an employee.

Also, he and I have a good history. He's always been cordial and very consistent in giving me good teaching schedules—a definite boon to my writing. In some respects I've thought of him as a friend. So I backed off from confrontation, made some vague, accommodating remarks which commit me to nothing, and these seemed to soothe him.

I do not intend to change one fucking thing I do in class. And my respect for Sir Gerald Minter has taken a bit of a nose dive. One more scholarly elitist with a rat turd for a brain. Our department's infested.


*Saturday, November 16*
Tonight as I study I hear rain sound. Through the window I see it's true, rain is falling, though not hard. It looks quite pretty under the streetlights. I watch for some time.

It has been many months since the last rain, I hope the rainy season begins. That's the way Los Angeles is, dry so much of the year, no rain at all, and then the rainy season.

In my homeland there is rainy season too, but much more rain than Los Angeles. During monsoon the rain comes almost every day. And our rain is strong, it roar on the roof and tear down leaves from trees. It rain so hard the world becomes dark and sometimes water cover the ground everywhere. The houses of the neighborhood look like they float on a lake.

I remember so well on rainy days mother would tell us stories, and let us help her make special sweets. When rain stop, Minh and me go outside and play.

61

We find big puddles in our yard and we like to wade in them barefeet. We sail little boats we make out of banana leaf. We save the drowning worms. After, we always take baths which is so nice on rainy day, I don't know why.

I am quite fond of the rain. To me Los Angeles would be better with more rain. Sometimes, here, even the rainy season seem dry.


*11/17/85*

What a difference a rain makes in this god forsaken urban wilderness.

Yesterday evening, before it rained, I walked up to the track to turn a few laps and found above me, in lieu of innocent sky, a violet radioactive sunset divided into three distinct layers of glowing particulate matter. Exhaust from the freeway hung heavy in the air. Not much better than sucking a tailpipe.

After two laps in that chemical soup I felt light-headed. My nose and throat burned. So did my eyes. I sat down on the infield, let my head clear. No need to asphyxiate myself in the name of athletic conditioning.

During the night came the rain. A trillion raindrops, nature's little miracle scrubbers, trapped the alien particles and dragged them back to earth—refining the atmosphere to pristine clarity.

When I ran this morning, the air (clover-fresh) slipped into my lungs and my legs moved almost of their own accord. The view out both ends of the stadium was amazing—so clear. To the south I could see the spans of the Vincent Thomas Bridge and 20 miles beyond to the gray hump of Catalina. North, the blue San Gabriels, chiseled and precise, looked so awfully close, their peaks lost in raincloud.

At a medium-fast pace I ran three miles for the first time in my life.

The magic of rain.

*Tuesday, November 19*

It is as I expect. I fail my essay on city vs. country. The grade is NC+. Teacher mention in his comments that when I argue both sides of issue I must use divided thesis. Such as: Personally, I find living in country and city equally attractive.

I feel so stupid because I remember how many times he tell us that in class. Why didn't I think of his words? I guess it's because I keep changing my mind how I will argue. Also, pressure. Always, when I write the English paper, I feel pressure.

On our next assignment I am more confident. It is a subject I know. The topic is: Should a college student work part-time job?

Here in U.S., always I work and go to school at same time, even in high school. Therefore I know exactly what I believe. My thesis will be, Yes, students should work, but no more than 20 hours per week, if possible.


*11/21/85*

When I went to class in RFK Hall today, all the escalators were running backward—backward mind you—much to the amusement of students and much to the annoyance of one elderly male faculty member. These escalators frequently break down. But the reversal of direction is a delightful new twist.

Jesus, the backward escalator—the perfect symbol for the screwed-up state of our entire campus. I mean, around Cal State, Maravilla, nothing works right. Nothing.

Take the clocks. I've heard that all of them are run from one master control, but if that's true the master controller is a lunatic with multiple personalities. I've seen clocks running fast, clocks running slow, clocks flying triple time, clocks skipping and jerking around the dial, and clocks not moving at all. What I rarely or perhaps never see is a clock with the correct time.

The typical CSUM classroom has a jammed thermostat, an overflowing trash can, two broken windows, a dirty stub of chalk, and a grabass platoon of broken-down, mismatched desks. The ersatz slate blackboard is warped into waves, the walls are peeling, the floor needs a sweep, and several overhead flourescent tubes are burned out. Another tube, on its way out, flickers with ominous buzz—inducing perturbation in unstable personalities.

The library of our alma mater houses a collection of missing books and vandalized magazines, a dozen malfunctioning copiers, and a vicious clique of surly librarians. We have a football stadium but no football team (the result of an NCAA death penalty), a cafeteria that gouges mercilessly for undercooked macaroni and cheese, and a campus bookstore with the slowest textbook orders in the western hemisphere, so slow that sometimes the course is half over before the books hit the shelves.

Then there's our caustic campus bureaucracy, our payroll office that siphons off employee pensions, and our high-octane president who screams at his male subordinates, tries to sleep with the female, and (according to rumor) is chauffeured home every day at 3:00 P.M. dead drunk in the back seat of his official limousine.

In these ways and others CSUM is the ghetto supermarket of college education.


*Sunday, November 24*
This morning when I get up I find Rayneece suitcase in the kitchen. Her door is open a little and I see her in bed sleeping.

I close her door and try to be quiet all day so I don't wake her. Now it is 11:00 pm and she is still asleep. She has been asleep for at least 16 hours.

I guess she didn't sleep much in Mexico.


*11/26/85*
Santa Anas have been blowing the past two days, sweeping hot, bone-dry air from the high desert into the city. It's been so uncomfortable at night I've had all the windows open, which is why last night I heard so clearly a loud moan, close by—apparently from Mr. Jazek's.

Not long ago another tenant was robbed and badly beaten in

her apartment, so I thought I'd better check. I pulled on my pants, went and knocked, asking through his door if he was okay.

Nothing for a time, then the old guy's voice. "I'm fine. Thanks, John." He sounded a little embarrassed.

Maybe his moan was from loneliness. Or maybe from the pressure of managing a declining property in a declining neighborhood. I don't think his life has been easy since he lost his wife. He's alienated half the tenants with his temper. Gets wasted every night, I think, but only at night.

He'd have opened the door if he wanted to talk. He talks to me more than anybody.

*Wednesday, November 27*

I was suppose to show Mr. Goddard my journal in class yesterday, let him count the pages I fill, but I forget to take it. So I go to his office today and we do it there.

I use this chance to ask him something bother me. Karen, my tutor, tell me English verbs will require long time to learn. It's because in Vietnam there are no verb tenses. If we want to say it happen yesterday, we say yesterday, and that's enough—who needs tenses? But English. So many tenses! And they don't even make sense!

So I ask him, if I can't learn English verb tenses by final, how can I pass?

My teacher say I must do my best to learn tenses, but more important write strong paper content, good clear arguments. If my content is strong, I can make some verb mistakes, still pass. I hope that's true. Hope he didn't say it just to push up my confidence.

He advice me same thing Karen say. If I want to learn English verbs better, I must read books written in English. Kindly, he offer me a book from his bookcase so I can start. It is call "The Old Man and the Sea."

I think this book will be easy to read. It has only 119 pages and the print is big. I look inside at some sentences and they are not difficult. Subject of book is old man go fishing and catch big fish. I will read over Thanksgiving.

Rayneece finally wake up after sleeping all day and all night. Now she is gone. She leave yesterday for Fresno where she spend Thanksgiving with her sister.

She did not have time to attend her classes.

*11/29/85*

Spooky new dream last night.

I'm on an overgrown jungle trail, alone. Thick canopy high above me chokes off sky and daylight.

I'm moving slow, loaded to the max with armaments. I'm a walking ammo dump. I've got an M-16, two holstered .45s, a grenade launcher, grenades, mortar rounds, Bowie knives and two bandoleers of rounds for the .50 caliber machine gun strapped to my back.

Despite my exemplary preparedness, my gut feels hollow. Close at hand is a sinister ticking I can't identify. None of my weapons should be ticking. What's ticking?

I realize with immense relief it's merely my watch, the ticking of my watch, amplified a hundredfold by my foolish fears. How amusing. Laughing at my idiocy, I watch the second hand sweep toward zero.

Zero? Why does the top of my watch read zero?!

As the hand reaches the goose egg, the ammo dump that is me answers my question by beginning to detonate. A grenade and a mortar round explode, blowing off an arm and a leg. Machine gun rounds ignite, clipping flesh, including my wienie. A grenade takes off one shoulder, another my head. When the world stops tumbling, from ground level I watch my guts fly forth wetly into the dirt.

At last the rolling thunder stops. The new me (the sentient me) seems to be my head, still alert. The rest of me looks dead. Feels dead too, there being no feeling.

"I" am resting on my left ear and cheek. I can see, about a yard from my face, a foot and attached calf standing upright in shoe and sock. Farther away is a hand missing its thumb. In the radius of my vision I see also a canteen, a liver, a ribcage, and of course the mass of entrails.

Well, in a way, this is good I'm thinking. I don't have to be anxious now or worry. I'm dying. I close my eyes, begin to relax, and it doesn't feel bad—to just relax and wait for it. What is life but pain, and what is death but eternal ease?

I become aware of stinging, a burning on the left side of my neck. Slowly it spreads to my cheek. It keeps spreading over my face like needle pricks, many, many needle pricks, and I'm wondering if it means I'm coming out of shock, waking to the pain throbbing in a billion blasted nerve ends.

Dangling in front of my eye is a struggling ant. It regains footing in my eyelash and continues on its way, climbing the shaky ladder. Others follow, pulling themselves clumsily upward, excited, trooping somewhere important on top of my head.

I am hyperconscious now and buzzing with anxiety. Death, I realize, could be far away. The whole left side of my face is blazing as the ants swarm over their new-found bounty, their community food chest.

Woke up then. Saw it was dark outside. Clock read 4:10. Though I needed more sleep, I knew I wouldn't get it. Showered, ate breakfast and worked on the novel. Put in three good hours before school.

*Saturday, November 30*
Mrs. Coberly call this morning to offer ride again. She think if I ride my bike I will be runned over or kidnap. It is nice of her to worry but I say again, really not necessary. Finally she give up. In result I have pleasant ride on beautiful day, get exercise too—and she don't have to drive which I know she dislike.

When I get there I learn she hire somebody new to keep house for her, like I did. Blanca is from Mexico. She's very young.

She is quite sweet girl and try hard to do everything right. However, there are things she doesn't know. She doesn't know American oven, dishwasher, microwave, just like me when I arrive.

She only speak English a little. She is insecure too, worser even than me.

Unfortunately, Mrs. Coberly does not always treat her with kindness. I see fear in Blanca's eyes. She is scare of mistakes, and of course Mrs. Coberly can be hard to please—though she can be nice too if she try.

Mostly I have good day over there, and wonderful turkey dinner with dressing, but when Mrs. Coberly ask me to stay all night, I explain I have studies.

"You study on vacation?" she ask, surprise.

I say yes, but I dont think she believe. Probably she think I got a guy to see. Once she tell me about her life in college and it seem like all she want to do is find a man. Naturally, it's hard for her to understand life of student like me.

I go home before dark so the cars can see me. I ride slow to look at all the different neighborhoods. I think, here I go—rich to poor this time. In just 7 mile, you see it all.

Where Mrs. Coberly live in San Marino almost every house is big, with big perfect lawn. There is much shade, many trees, bushes, flowers. The streets are wide and clean. Not much traffic, almost no people, except somebody come out of house to drive a car. Old people usually.

But as I ride my bike the houses get smaller, lawns not so big or pretty, streets not so wide, less trees. Now in the yards I see more people, children too. There is more traffic and sometimes trash in the street, as never in San Marino. The cars go faster, I have to be more careful, ride close to the curb.

Near where I live the houses are tiny or else they are divide up into apartments. Some dont have a yard, some do, but the yards are mostly dirt. Trees—forget it. Well, maybe a few. People are everywhere, on porches, yards, even standing on street talking. Kids are everywhere too. Playing, riding bikes, roller skating. Elders are on the sidewalk going someplace or sitting on their porches watching.

This makes me wander: which is better, green and peaceful neighborhood with no people—or poor, dirty neighborhood full of people? What a choice. Too bad you can't have pretty neighborhood with people, that's my opinion. It was like that in my old neighborhood in Can Tho when I was a girl. We didn't know we are lucky.

In the evening, I decide to begin the book Mr. Goddard give me. I am thinking I can read most of it before I go to bed.

At first I like it a lot. It is about this old man who fishes and a boy who helps. They want to fish together as in the past, but they cant because the boy's father says no. The father feel the old fisher use up all his luck, and will never catch another fish.

Therefore the old man sail by himself far from land. The writer describe the sea so real you begin to think you are there on the water under the sun with waves rocking the boat. Somehow I can smell the sea and the rotten fish stink in the boat.

Then I begin to get sick. Sick to my stomach, but also the memories of the shrimp boat come back, and I see everything exactly as it happen when those bad fishers kill my poor dad. The more I try to read, the more I see that awful stuff.

I don't believe I can finish the book. But I must think of something to tell my teacher, because probably he will ask did I like it.


*12/2/85*

The 002 final reading materialized in my box today like a black fungus. It's a ballbuster—a very theoretical piece by Theodore Yeoman, "The Death of the American Family." He argues that the traditional nuclear family of western culture is becoming obsolete as a result of social and economic changes over the past 500 years.

The guy develops an interesting case, but to understand it one needs background in European social history since the Renaissance and a graduate student's vocabulary, both rare among basic writing students. Much of the essay is ironic, and that can be quite misleading to those from cultures in which irony is not a common mode of written expression. They're apt to take ironic statements at face value.

Such problems in the reading (and no doubt others I don't yet see) will generate confusion, and when the students are confused, not sure what to say, their writing quality collapses at all levels—

content, syntax, grammar. Many will flunk this final, that is certain. If the exam question turns out to be as putrid as the reading, we'll have a blood bath.

Thrust upon us is a situation that cries out for "coaching." Yet we're not supposed to coach, right? Planning or coincidence?

Remember this: In the shadow of the Hump, there is no coincidence.


*Tuesday, December 3*

Today Mr. Goddard give us reading for final exam. It seem very difficult to me, something about American families fading away.

He try hard to explain the reading to us. He write things on board, wave his arms in air, talk and talk, but I sit thinking just one thing: If this is our reading for the final, I will fail, no doubt.

Usually when we have a new reading, the class ask many question, argue and discuss. But today we are silent. Only Araceli speak, with anger in her voice. She ask Mr. Goddard who pick the reading.

He admit it is very bad reading. He is angry too, he say, like us. Then he write on blackboard name of lady who pick reading: Professor Mary Parcell. He tell us, after final is over we should complain to the boss of Professor Mary Parcell—Dean of Liberal Arts. Then he write Dean's name, address on board. Mr. Goddard say we must protest unfairness of exam, only way to help the students next semester get a better reading. "The system here will never improve," he preach us, "unless you guys get involve."

Unfortunately, I feel defeated when teacher say those things. Maybe he is correct, I'm thinking, but how is complaining to anybody going to help me pass? By the time I complain, I will not be Cal State student. Will they listen to some dumb girl who flunk out?

I notice our whole class is in bad mood. Teacher ask questions, but nobody answer, just stare at him like drop dead. Finally, he let us go early, I think because he can't get nobody to talk.

He stop me to tell me my narrative "Minh and Dao" will be publish. A magazine here on campus will publish it, in the spring. The magazine has strange name—Paved River Review.

"I wont be here in spring," I say, then leave before he can add one word. It is very rude I know, but my feelings are so strong at the time I cant help it.

At home I find Rayneece is back, she notice I clean the apartment. However, no thanks from her. Soon as I walk in, she start criticizing. Why? She don't like the Happy Carpet I buy and sprinkle on the beer spots her friends make. She say the chemicals stink worse than the beer, and they poison the environment, us too probably.

I apologize, to keep the peace, but she make me so angry. Kind acts I do for her are a waste, forget it.


*12/4/85*
The 002 final reading is a disaster. The students don't understand it, they hate it, and they're beginning to hate me for trying to teach it. Yet if I don't, they'll all fail.

The reading chosen for 101 is also proving problematic. The issue there—whether drugs should be legalized—is only working with those students who are drug users, or have been. Those with no drug experience are in most cases constructing virulent knee-jerk moralistic blasts of illogic. Many believe that casual marijuana users should be jailed and cokeheads electrocuted, for the preservation of democracy. In other words they parrot our politicians and the media.

Thanks to the Humper these past three days have been—hands down—the worst of my teaching career. And we're just fucking getting started.


*Thursday, December 5*
When I go to English today, I see note tape on classroom door: MR. GODDARD'S CLASS IS CANCELLED.

I stand there, feeling very scare, as others arrive. We discuss about the note.

Most think no big deal, Mr. Goddard is just sick and will come back next time. Some even smile, happy to be free.

But two people think like me, that the note is bad news. We believe our teacher will not miss class now, with the final so close, unless the reason is serious. If he is sick, he must be very sick.

*12/7/85*
Somewhat busted up.
   Car accident—3 days ago I think.
   My case caused a big shit fit here at the hospital. For some reason they couldn't locate the emergency contacts listed with my employer. It was as though Robert Gadzooks of Crosspatch, Arkansas and Sarah Barndip of Peameadows, Belgium didn't even exist.
   The staff called Mr. Jazek, who used his pass key to search my place, looking for a relative's address. Again no luck, but then I regained consciousness so the whole relatives issue became moot. As it turned out they didn't need to open my bean after all.
   Mr. Jazek, standup dude. He has trouble driving after dark, but drove down last night to bring me the essentials, including a get-well gift: a pint of vodka. Showed me how nicely the flat bottle stows under a pillow.
   Didn't ask about the accident. Not a word.
   I won't forget this.

*Sunday, December 8*
Rayneece not have one date since she come back from her sister. Guys call, but she makes some excuse and gets off the phone. She stay in her room with the door close most of the day. However, there is no crying. She play music, but not loud.
   In our kitchen are many new foods which she buy: pretzels, potato chips, nuts, crackers, twinkies, etc. In the refrigerator are potato salad, chop veggies, onion dip, oranges, grapes. In the freezer, popsickles and three boxes of ice cream.
   I think maybe she is studying in her room, because when she come out last time, for carrot sticks, I see this book open on her desk next to her coke. Is it a school book? I can't see. But it's big enough.

*12/9/85*

Don't remember the accident. Last I recall I was on the Pasadena Freeway doing about 60, everything under control. Then I flashed back to a very bad night in 1969.

We were lifting some wounded civilians out of a delta village under heavy small arms fire. When the chopper was about 50 feet up, our pilot caught a round above his ear and slumped forward onto the joystick.

We listed to the right, nose turning down, and fell. With the floor pitched forward all anyone could do was hang on as we sank back through the treetops toward the up-zooming grass. When we hit, we flew forward into the collapsing, shattering nose. Three of the wounded died, along with the pilot. The rest of us got fucked up pretty bad.

I went through all that again, as helpless as before, while a totally different scenario unfolded in front of witnesses on the freeway. They say I drifted left through two lanes of traffic, jumped the curb and flipped, vaulting the restraining fence and dropping 15 feet into a concrete drainage ditch. The car hit grill first, approximately. The cops say my seatbelt saved me, but not by much. One of the anchor bolts tore through the floor.

Cundiff's Mustang is totalled beyond any car restorer's most absurd fantasy, and it's really a shame. That beast was one of the sweetest, best-maintained 352s still on the road.

I knew Cundiff should have never picked me to honor in his will, not with a car. I'm wrath of God on anything with four wheels. Moto-Shiva.

But I guess he didn't have anyone else.


*Tuesday, December 10*

A substitute teach us in English today, Mr. Franklin. He say Mr. Goddard involve in car accident, hurt himself so bad he cant come back all semester.

I am stun, miserable. All in class feel the same I think. It's like bomb drop. While we sit, Mr. Franklin walk around the class, put a paper on our desk.

"What's this?" Araceli ask.

"It's a poem," he say.

"A poem? What for?"

Our new teacher's eyes look surprise behind his glasses. "We're going to read and discuss it."

"Why?" she demand.

Now he look annoy. "Because that's what I plan for today's class."

Then Mariko raise her hand. "What about the final reading?" she ask in her sweet voice.

"What final reading?"

Several people groan. I look around the class, see hate in many eyes.

Mariko explain to him, very polite, show him the reading.

He take it and read for some minutes. "This is your final reading?" he ask.

More groans.

He explain that nobody tell him about final reading, so how can he know? He's only the substitute isn't he? He say he will ask his boss about it. Also he will study the reading, meet with us next class to discuss. Then he let us go, which I think is good since he have nothing useful to teach.

*12/11/85*

This morning I learned the diagnostic staff decided to keep me another week for "observation." Because of the headaches. Headaches? What the fuck do they expect after a concussion? Of course I have headaches. No new hemorrhaging shows on the CT scan and the swelling is normal, so it's pretty clear the worst is over. The docs are just being safe to cover their fannies.

I gave the resident on duty so much flak he summoned Dr. Shrivastiva, Chief of Diagnostics, a Napoleonic figure with considerably more taste for debate than his younger colleague.

"You were in a coma a few days ago, Mr. Goddard. If you get up, walk around, pursue normal activities, you may be in one again very soon."

"My problem."

"Everyone's problem."

"I'll sign whatever releases you want. Absolve you and the hospital of all responsibility."

"We can't release you. You're not out of danger."

"You're just trying to bleed my insurance carrier."

That got to him, I could see. His soft brown eyes hardened. "You don't wish to learn what caused you to lose consciousness on the freeway? Almost killing yourself, endangering other motorists as well?"

"I already know."

He stared at me.

"I was daydreaming about Minnie Mouse. Shot a wad and fainted."

He was trying not to lose his temper, but I'd brought him to the edge.

"Can I go?"

"And the headaches?"

"I can handle the headaches. Give me some pills."

He finally agreed, just to get rid of me I think, and made me sign a sheaf of releases. I thought he'd keep me on the Darvons for another week, but when I asked, he smiled and began writing on his prescription pad. "Darvon is highly addictive, Mr. Goddard, and now that you're feeling so chipper there is no need. Two aspirin every six hours, no more."

He tore off the prescription, handed it to me and departed, the princely little shit. I wadded it up and bounced it off his back.

Aspirin?!!

After they fitted me with a cane, and while I was waiting for the cab, the last of the codeine was deserting me and the pain (never far away) began to grip my skull again. Felt it in the ankle too. Slipped into the restroom and tapped the vodka to dull it down.

On the way home we stopped by Dick's Cottage Pharmacy so I could fill three prescriptions written by Dr. John. Darvon isn't the last word in pain relief, after all, and at Dick's money talks.

Oh, Yesssssssss....

*Thursday, December 12*

Big surprise! When I go to English today, Mr. Goddard stand in front of class. He has bandage on head, cast on foot. In his hand is stick to help him limp.

He apologize to us for missing. He say he come down with freeway flu, which make us laugh because it is so dumb. I'm sure the others feel like me—glad to have our teacher back.

Then he say "O.K. let's get to work!"

We work hard all class as he help us understand the reading by Yeoman. First we study each paragraph together, summarize the main points of author's meaning. Second, we discuss the reading, try to find out what position we each will take on author's argument. Then we divide in groups to answer ten questions Mr. Goddard give us concerning the reading.

I take many notes today, study them after class. Already I feel more confident because I think I understand Yeoman's main ideas now. As I study more, I will understand even better.

After class, several of us help our teacher carry his things. In the sunlight, he look quite tired and pale. I see he is not well at all. I find I feel guilty for putting suspicion on him before. Also, last time I see him I show such disrespect. Now he risk his health for us.

In his office, Mariko ask can we help while he is recovery?

At first he's hesitate. But he mention that typing is hard for him now, because he gets headaches.

I am fast and accurate typer ever since high school. So I offer. Mariko too. It is only few hours work, easy if we divide.

Mr. Goddard want to pay us, but I am not comfortable taking money, and Mariko feel same. We argue this way. Since he help us in class so much, why we can't help him back? He see our point and agree to let us do it for free.

*12/12/85*

Minter gave my 002 sections to Lawrence Franklin, one of the new hires. I met the guy in the mailroom a couple months back and got the impression of a breezy, self-confident Phid kid.

Called old Larry last night to thank him for standing in and to let him know I'd be back today to take over.

Well, he was reluctant to step down. Told me Minter had promised the classes to him for the rest of the semester. Also, he's done the lesson plans already and feels he's hit it off with the students. According to him, everything's tootling along just peachy without me.

Now we all know the only reason someone would take on extra classes is for extra money. And since it's for the money, I knew Franklin wouldn't give a shit whether my students passed or not. Besides, he's too green.

I told him he was welcome to sit in with us but made clear I'd be teaching the class, and if he challenged my authority or became disruptive in any way, I'd be forced to deal with him in the manner appropriate.

He didn't show today, so I guess my word to the wise penetrated.

A terrific headache's been banging since early afternoon. Can't seem to dull it down. Feeling numbed out and dopey. Productive work is impossible, so bed is probably the best move. I won't sleep, but I can doze, get a little rest.


*Friday, December 13*
Today at work, Robert take practice test in his GRE study guide. After he finish, I ask how he did.

He will not say his scores. But he tell me he got quite high in numerical, low in verbal. He look unhappy.

"Your science major," I tell him. "Verbal is not important."

He explain that the schools he apply to do not take people with any big weakness. Even physics student must have high verbal to compete.

Well, maybe he's right. But why apply to best schools only? That is not smart in my opinion because maybe none will pick you.

He show me this formula he derive. He plan to use it to guess on the multiple choices. His formula is clever and will get him some points I believe, but it cannot change low verbal score to high one.

I was right, Rayneece is studying. This morning when she shower, she leave some xeroxes on the coffee table and I see they are pages copy from somebody's notebook.

Now I know why she doesn't go to class. She has a friend who makes it easy for her. Wonder if it's a guy. Can't really tell from the writing.

*12/15/85*

It's depressing to know my eyes have only about four hours of good work in them a day. When I push beyond that the world blurs and a booming headache descends, worse the harder I push.

Teaching and paper grading consume all my productive hours; zilch time for the story collection. The irony is I've got tons of idle time on my hands because often I'm too ill to do anything but vegetate. Very frustrating.

Also, I'm drinking too much.

My torporous funk came to a head last night when physician heal thyself backfired. I became overmedicated in the kitchen and passed out on my feet. I was reaching to open the refrigerator and next I knew I was falling backward into the wastebasket and wall. Lucky I didn't hit my head. Might have been a problem.

Today, my usual bronco-size headache carries on its back a righteous hangover, spurring and whooping like a cowpoke.

*Monday, December 16*

Since two weeks, my physics lab partner is ditching class and lab. I call her dorm many times but Carrie is never there. I leave three message with her roommate. No call back until tonight.

Carrie say she so sorry—cough, cough, cough—she got walking newmonia and is too sick to call before. She say she want to help on our semester project, but maybe only a little because she feel very, very sick. She can't risk her health just for a grade, as she explain. Then she cough some more.

I think Carrie's lazy, and she knows I want good grade. She knows I will do all the work myself, just to be sure of get an A.

But I figure her out too. I always know she can let me down and that's why I keep the notebook with our tabulations and graphs. I can do this project by myself, no problem, and with Carrie's help my chance for good grade would be less. She is not careful.

As we discuss it, I agree to do the calculations and write report, and she will correct my grammars and find typist. She will pay typist too. I think she keep this promise because her part is so easy.

All day Rayneece type in her room, from before noon to now— 1:00 am. She is not fast, but she never stop except for food. Obviously she knows how to work.


*12/16/85*

Couldn't get the rental car started this morning. Found myself limping speedily to campus on the cane. I must have presented quite a sight to onlookers. Best exercise I've had since the accident, though I sweated through my shirt and got a little dizzy.

Tonight the thundering headache is back, banging. Even music grates. Would love to be able to bonk my skull a few times on the wall, just to vary the pain.


*Tuesday, December 17*

This afternoon I help Mr. Goddard in his office by typing questions for his 101 students. He make them up, tell me, and I type. That way he save his eyes. Much of the time he keep eyes close.

Sadly, he look sicker today than last time. His hands shake. When he try to drink coffee, he spill some on his leg. I ignore, but feel bad. Obviously it's not wise what he's doing. He should lie on bed, get well.

The typewriter in his office is old manual, not easy to use, but typing only take an hour because there isn't much. Does he have more work for me, I ask. No he say, Mariko did the rest.

I guess he notice I'm a little disappoint. "You know about word processors?" he ask. He explain that his book will be publish soon, and publisher want it on discs. Maybe I can advise him what to do.

"Why dont you use word processor in computer lab?" I offer. "I show you how to do it, help if you have trouble."

But he say no, he must hire typist because of his eyes.

"Typist can come to computer lab."

Then I get better idea. I will be working less hours over break—as Robert tell me last week. And I wont have no homeworks. I can input my teacher's book. Why not? I'm a fast typer.

But Mr. Goddard say no, no, oh no, he can't do that. That would be taking advantage of me. Impossible.

We argue back and forth till finally I get him to let me do it—for money. He believe by pay me, then he does not take advantage, and it's okay.

Why argue? On his face is this sincere look. I know if I insist, he will find somebody else, somebody he can pay.

Even though it will take long hours, I want to help him with his book. Maybe later many students will study it. Dr. Parviz write the book he use for our class, and it's good one. I am proud to be involve in something like that.

Therefore I let him believe I will accept his money.


*12/17/85*

Feeling low tonight, really low—tired, demoralized, depressed.

Beginning to worry about habituation to the Percodan. Been eating them like candy. Dr. John is switching me to Tylenol tomorrow. We'll see.


*Wednesday, December 18*

I arrive to English final exam 10 minutes early, but already cafeteria is fill with students, I see no place to sit. Phuong and Mariko wave at me and I join them at their table.

Mariko put her whiteout in middle so we all can use. In front of me I place my grammar book, dictionary, two pens. Below I put the scratch paper they give us, and the exam paper we must use. This paper is so strange to me. Each line we write on has four little boxes at the end. Mariko say its where they add up our mistakes.

We wait some minutes with nothing to do, getting more nervous. Both my classmates look scared and pale, I must look same. At 9:00, the teachers hand out test question and test begin.

At first, the question look easy to me, because it ask whether we agree with Yeoman that the family has changed its structure as result of social, economic, and historical forces. That I can answer. But there are more words in question, and these confuse me. They say I must explain what effect the new style of family will have on future society. Also, I must illustrate my arguments with personal experiences.

How crazy, I'm thinking. I can't understand present American society, so how I guess future? And how to use my personal experiences to illustrate? *My* family is me and some ghosts.

Then I think, maybe question has deeper level. So I read it more times, but I do not see deeper level. That's when I notice both Mariko and Phuong have their dictionaries open. Mariko is writing Japanese characters next to words she circle in test question. Phuong is doing same in Vietnamese.

They make me realize I forget the important advice Mr. Goddard tell us many times: every word you don't understand, look it up in dictionary.

I circle all words in the question which are not clear to me, then look up each one, write out the definitions. Unfortunately, most of the words have more than one meaning. And even with the definitions, the question still confuse me.

Thirty minutes are gone now and my friends are both writing their essays. Suddenly I feel panic. I calm myself by breathing slow, say to myself, it is only a test, only a test.

I read question one more time, concentrate hard as I can, and still I dont understand the last part. But I decide I must write something. No time for outline. I just write.

I begin by agree with Yeoman, and explain in my words what he say. For examples, I create fake family, with a divorce mom and divorce dad and my two little step-brothers. I try to write fast, to catch up with my classmates, but I am nervous and make many mistakes, which I have to stop and whiteout. I know time is passing, but its like a bad dream. The harder I try to go fast, the slower I go. Soon only 10 minutes remain.

To answer last part of question, I just guess. I scribble one paragraph about what can happen to families in future, like babies will be born from test tube, state will raise the babies without parents, family love will disappear, and most people will live in small apartment alone, or in gangs. Since no one will care about anybody, crime will be much higher. There will be many suicides, I say.

Some of this I make up, and some come from this book I read in high school, "Brave World." As I try to think of conclusion for my essay, a teacher yell "Time's up."

Already this lady stand beside me, waiting, as I write one sentence for conclusion: "In future, the family will be different in many ways." Then I give her my exam. I walk out of cafeteria feeling horrible, sure I fail.

Outside, Phuong and Mariko wait for me. They ask how I did. As we discuss, it shock us to learn that we interpret the last part of test question three different ways. Its like our ideas are from different planets. Which suggest that if one of us pass, the other two must fail.

However, I think all of us will fail. Like me, Mariko will have to leave school. For Phuong, this is her first try at 002. She can wait to fail college next semester.

All day, since the test, I feel miserable. I feel why study for my other finals, because I'm out of school. I stare at TV and feel sorry for myself. Dont even know what I watch.

*12/18/85*

The 002 final was a bloody raving werewolf. The exam question was unclear, mindless, nearly unanswerable. Since it may be the stupidest test question ever posed, I offer it here for posterity:

Yeoman maintains that the contemporary family is manifesting "structural metamorphosis to the point of new identity under certain critical and irreversible social, economic, and historical forces." Do you agree with his interpretation of family change, and what impacts and implications do you envision for future society and our family values? Explain in a coherent well-organized essay of at least 600 words. Be sure to illustrate your position with personal experiences.

I smelled blood bath as soon as I read it, and that's proving to be the case. At our instructors' meeting after the test we failed six of eight sample pulls. The failing students had in all cases suffered near total logical and linguistic collapse.

I took the opportunity to point out that the problems we were finding in the exams had been caused by the test question more than anything else. I explained the worst snags I saw.

MHP listened, smiling, eyes icy, until I was done. She looked around the table. "Anyone else feel the question was too difficult?"

"Some of my students told me afterward they felt challenged by it," said Ann Cowley. "But no one complained. They like being challenged."

Chris Siefert reported that his students liked both the Yeoman reading and the test question. He couldn't imagine what I was talking about.

"Two of my students had a little trouble," said Lawrence Franklin, smirking as he avoided my eyes, "but those two haven't understood anything all semester."

And, from the silent majority, silence as usual.

Then Randy Kastor spoke up. "Most of my students didn't understand the question, including the brightest ones. Their responses are everywhere."

"I see," said the Hump. "Did the question seem too difficult to you?"

Randy blinked. "It seemed difficult for basic writing students. Might be more appropriate in freshman comp."

"But did it seem unfair?"

His eyes fluttered around the table for support, got none other than mine, and it wasn't enough. He expelled breath. "Not unfair, I suppose, but extremely challenging. So challenging I don't expect many of my students will pass."

Ignoring his dig, the Humper smiled brightly. "Anyone else?" Subject closed.

I've been grading all afternoon and evening, trying to give the students every possible break. If an essay has even minimal coherence and fluency, I pass it, because for basic writers, on this assignment, that's all anyone could reasonably ask.

Still, with half the exams graded, I've failed almost 70%. Never seen it this bad. Never.

*Saturday, December 21*

Carrie surprise me a little—she flake out completely. She won't even answer my phone calls. Finally, I type the report myself because deadline arrive.

But I decide she can't get away with it. On top of the report I put my name only, then attach note to Dr. Massarotti, explain what happen. Carrie needs to learn more than Tina is a fool.

Rayneece has finish her finals, I believe. She stay up more nights than me this week, now is catching up on her sleep. Wish I could sleep like her.

All my tests are finish, but I dont think I did good on them. Hard to concentrate. I must decide what to do when I leave CSUM.

*12/23/85*

Got the composition finals back today. The 101s did better than I expected (about 70% passed), but the scene in 002 was really bad. Of my 30 students in both classes, 23 failed (initially at least), including some of the best writers.

My impulse was to pack my .45 up to campus and unload a clip into the witch, cartwheeling her across her office floor.

Then I thought of something better.

When I filled in my 002 grade roster for section 11, I passed two of the failed students by bubbling in CR next to their names.

Since no one can change my official grades except me, the passes should stand.

I had to pass Araceli. She's one of the best argumentative writers I've ever worked with, one of the best writers period. And Tina Le, though not as well rounded, has an amazing gift for narrative, truly exceptional. I mean she's had a story accepted by our school literary magazine and I'm supposed to fail her in Basic Writing II?

Of course there were others that deserved to pass, at least a dozen, but the problem was, their papers during the course were merely competent, never outstanding (A+ level). If later I have to defend my buccaneer passes, I'll need papers like Araceli's "Country Life" and Tina's "Minh and Dao." No one could doubt that the authors of those deserve to pass 002.

Should be fun. MHP and Minter are going to fart blue thunder. If I can change grades—and they can't stop me—it means anyone can change grades. Revolution by grade bubble, baby.

Need to call Tina and Araceli to tell them what I did. They should be prepared for what may come. I don't think the Department can do anything to them, but you never know.


*Monday, December 23*
Strange day. I wake up feel so bad. Even though vacation begin, I cant think anything except how I fail English.

At 11 am Mr. Goddard call. He tell me I pass English 002! Can you believe how happy I feel? To know for sure I fail, then find out I pass? My heart almost jump out of me.

"How did I pass final?" I ask him, because I can't believe it.

Hmm, Hmm, well, he say, you didn't exactly pass final.

My heart sink down again. As I listen, I find out he write CR next to my name on his grade form, even though I flunk final. And why did he do it? He must do it, he say, because I am such fine writer, surely dont deserve to fail his course.

"Did you pass other students—same way as me?"

Just Araceli, he say.

Araceli? How could she fail? She is top student in our class.

"She had trouble with the question," he explain. "Tried to attack it with logic."

"Did anybody in our class pass the final?"

"In your class, only four," he say.

So few? It shock me. "Did Phuong and Mariko pass?" I ask him.

"No they didn't."

I want to ask more, but I'm afraid to know that all my friends fail. It make me feel shame. I should fail too, except for kindness of my teacher.

After I hang up, Rayneece ask who call. I can see she's curious, maybe because she hear his voice when she answer the phone—a man's voice.

"My English teacher."

"Oh," she say, disappoint. She ask his name and I tell her, but she don't know him.

As we discuss I learn she fail English 002 and English 101, each one time. She thank God she finally finish her English requirement and manage to stay in school. "Is your teacher any good?" she ask.

"Yes."

"Your lucky. That department has some real lulus."

All day I consider why Mr. Goddard pass me, and now I believe I understand. He wants to fight the injustice system, try to make it fair. That is honorable path, especially in America, where such actions are accepted. I just worry because he see it so simple.

He say there is nothing English department can do about our grades, now that he change them. But I wander. The department is more powerful than him aren't they?


*12/25/85*

Been working on the stories as much as possible. Not making major changes. Don't have time. Besides, I wrote the yarns when I was a diaper butt. The only way I can re-enter anything like that callow mindset is through Corporal Ernest Candide—and that would inject an unwanted sardonic tone.

Mainly I'm trying to find and correct such jarring implausibilities of human behavior and natural fact as I occasionally come across. Also doing a lot of line tightening. The style is a snap—being almost pure Hemingway. I wrote under that spell for so many years I can do it in my sleep.

Adding irony where appropriate. Irony comes to me easily these days and it provides needed ballast to the facile Hemingway surface structure. Nobody knew that better than Papa.

*Thursday, December 26*
I spend Christmas day with Mrs. Coberly. For dinner she invite nine guest, only six come. She find this quite upsetting. Two guests especially irritate her because they don't even bother to call. And so Mrs. Coberly take out her anger on Blanca.

Example: when Blanca bring in the ham and Mrs. Coberly find it slice too thick she say "What did you cut it with, Blanca, an ax?"

Blanca is so embarrass. She pick up the ham, take it back to the kitchen to try again. I go help her because I know how Mrs. Coberly like it, slice thin as paper. Blanca watch me, eyes full of fear like always, then she cut some too. This time, Mrs. Coberly accept.

Later, when Blanca and I do dishes, I try to talk to her a little, as best as I can (she doesn't know too much English, and I can't speak Spanish). She say she work all day, seven days a week, but only get same money as I did. That doesn't seem fair, because I was always student when I live with the Coberlys. I didn't work full time except in summer.

Blanca doesn't go to school, even though she's only 15. She's learning English quite slowly—mostly such words as wash, cook, clean, why did you do that?, do it again.

Her family is in Mexico but she can't go back there and live with them. They need her to earn money in the U.S., to support them. Blanca and her sister are the main money earners in their family. She tell me why but I didn't understand.

Blanca is illegal, therefore she feel she must accept Mrs. Coberly's unkind words and small pay. She belief if she make some big mistake or complain too much, Mrs. Coberly will call the Immigration.

I understand Mrs. Coberly needs a person she can depend on, but this is not good way to make a relationship. If she treat Blanca in more human manner, then trust can grow between them, maybe friendship. Blanca will serve willingly, perhaps she can stay many years. As Mrs. Coberly learn yesterday, she does not have as many friends as she think. Can she afford to make Blanca her enemy?

If someone serve your needs, it is not wise to make them hate or mistrust you. How can you gain from their bad feelings inside your house?


*12/27/85*
Bought a car today, a 1970 Ford Galaxy in pretty good mechanical shape. The blue paint is faded from fifteen years of street parking and there's some rust in the cooling system but it should be a good around-the-town car. Fords die hard.

Bought it from a woman at Mr. Jazek's cathedral. Her husband passed away in November and he was the one who drove it. Didn't drive it much. The odometer says 55,000 and from the pedal and seat wear I'd say it's for real.

The only problem is my new insurance premium. The crooks want $3743 a year—and that's for minimum liability only! At that astronomical rate I'd have to make monthly payments, which would jack the total to over four fucking grand! For a two-grand car.

I just couldn't convince the peckerwood it matters much that no one except me has ever been injured in any of my accidents. They've all been solo affairs. True, I've wiped out some lightpoles, barrels, fences, trees and the like, but I've never hurt anybody, my insurance from work has picked up all my medical tabs, and the total property damage I've caused is maybe ten thousand (excluding my cars). For this, they want four fucking grand a year to cover me?

He points out sarcastically that the Calamity Jack policy he's offering insures just three small groups: Hollywood stunt drivers, motorized daredevils and me. Claims no other carrier would even touch me.

I hung up on the bastard. I mean, a man does his best to

comply with the law, but only to the point of self-nullification. I can't afford four grand a year. The time has come to operate my vehicle without insurance.

Hell, my savings in the first six months will pay off the new wheels. Why didn't I think of this before?

*Saturday, December 28*
Last night two girls I know in high school come by to visit. They are home for break. Jennifer go to Stanford now. Claudia is at Notre Dame.

In high school, I was not exactly friends with them, but sort of. There was too much competition at Blessed Sacrament for friendship to be deep. Also, I was so different from the other girls. I was three years older, come from different country, speak English with horrible accent, and I'm fake Catholic too.

The way I look back then, oh my god, with my hair just one inch long and my body so skinny my dress hang on me like close umbrella. One day in the bathroom I overhear three girls talking and learn my nickname. Boat Girl. Accurate, I suppose.

Of course when I meet Jennifer, it is a little different. Because I think maybe we can be friends. One reason is she has Asian blood (her Mom is Chinese). More important, it seem like inside her eyes I see this very sweet, innocent, scared girl looking out. It was that inside person I want to know, and maybe be friends.

But it didn't happen. When I try to talk to her, she speak to me with others around, but is uncomfortable to be alone with me, just us two together. She is such a polite person it took me weeks to know this for sure. But finally I realize the truth. When it's only the both of us, people think she's Asian, and she don't want that.

I can't blame her. She grow up her whole life in U.S.A. This is her culture and she must fit in. However, it means we can only be friendly, never friends. Even last night, which was nice, I was thinking did she and Claudia visit because they like me, or is it because I go to state college and they can feel superior?

When I was in Vietnam, friendship was not so difficult for me.

As a child, I have many friends. What I miss the most is friends like those, friends I care about, who care about me. Friends who always try to put themselves on equal level, never above in superior position.

Sometimes I think there must be people out there who can be my friend, but their probably the same as me. Instead of going places and having fun and meeting each other, they sit home writing in journal and feel sorry for themself.

Trust is necessary to make a friend, and maybe it is impossible for me to trust people. Sometimes I think that's my problem. That my problem is me. Maybe it's those things that happen to me years ago.

Rayneece is spending break with her mother in Inglewood. She leave Monday afternoon in a big hurry, say she have to pick up sister at the airport. She ask me to take her library books back to library because she don't have time. I agree, but really I feel she should of did it herself. Doesn't she have car?

*12/30/85*

Tina works most mornings so we'll be inputting from 1:00 to 5:00, as we did today. Wanted to do two stories, but after we decided on the margins, the page numbers, the font, the pitch and all that, we had time for only one.

I picked "The Seedling" to go first because the changes are so minor. It's a simple tale, no pretensions, little need for ironic flavoring. Don't really like it much—too syrupy for my present taste—but it does contribute to the book.

Tina's a fast and accurate typist. I felt it went quite well, except for one thing. Her supervisor, Robert (on duty in the afternoons), seems to have taken an aversion to me. From the time we were introduced till he left he ignored me with a vengeance.

Tina says he's immature. Apparently such behavior is normal.

*Monday, December 30*

Today I learn Mr. Goddard is *not* writing book for school. It is only stories—short stories he call them. They concern a teenager boy. I am a little disappointment that the book is not for college students. Also, it seem odd to me, a book of stories.

"Who will read it?" I ask.

Oh, people who like stories, he say.

I guess there are a lot in America. When he tell me that, I begin to feel better. What we do is important, I think, even though I do not completely understand. Also, I find I like the story we do today. It is about when the boy decides to be a writer.

I like how story is written, but what I like best is relationship between the boy and his mother. She's the one give him his interest in books and writing. She read him many stories when he is little, make him fall in love with words, dreams, fantasies, as he say, long before he start school.

Mom is sensitive woman and she pass this along to her son. Always protect the misfortunate ones, she teach. Don't ever be a bully. The strong love between these two is quite beautiful I think. I must wander, can it be about my teacher when he's a boy and his mother? Kind of hard to imagine, because he does not seem sentimental. But I think maybe.

Now I understand why my teacher praise "Minh and Dao." In U.S., stories are respected. They go in books for adults to read. When I write my story, I didn't even know what I'm doing. I consider it only a English paper.

Robert act quite strange today. He try to freeze us completely. Also, he leave without one word to me, which he never did before.

His behavior is so rude Mr. Goddard ask about it, and I didn't exactly say the truth. I tell him Robert act like that all the time. I don't want my teacher to be uncomfortable working in lab, or feel like he's making a problem. He has as much right to use lab as anybody. It belongs to the university, not Robert.

I don't know what Robert is thinking, but he will have to get use to us. I will be helping my teacher many more days.

*Advent of the New Year*

Already I hear outdoors the snap, crackle and pop of fireworks and guns—yet my watch (quite accurate) reads 11:58. It's the premature ejaculators, folks.

'Tis not the hour to be strolling the street, with M-80s KER-BOOMing and lead whizzing down from the sky. Dogs crawl under beds and babies cry. In jigs the infant year, tiny face wrinkled and sly.

Happy bitching 1986. Year of the Warthog.


*Wednesday, January 1*

This morning I write to Julie, my advisor at Songkhla Refugee Camp in Thailand. She is nicest American I know, a very kind woman and good friend. Me and the other girls in Songkhla we call her in Vietnamese "auntie," and that is exactly how she treat us all—as her nieces.

We need such a person because we are in such bad condition when we arrive. Physically most of us are wrecks, from many days without food and water. But the main injury is to our spirit. For weeks I am so depress I can not eat, don't want to talk, never smile or laugh. Like most of the new girls, I spend the day inside my own mind remembering just the things I want to forget.

Even now, sometimes, I am like that. This side of me Julie knows so well. She is the only person I ever tell what happen to me on the island, most of it.

I hope my letter will reach. She did not answer the one I send in July, I don't know if she receive. Her address is changing frequently, I worry she has move and forget to tell me.


*1/2/86*

Rained off and on the entire cold, dripping, gloomy day. It was raining when Tina and I knocked off, so I gave her a lift home.

She lives three blocks north of campus (and four blocks south of me) in a well-maintained old frame house that's been subdivided.

She and a roommate have half of the second floor. Looks like a nice place, though the street generally is a little run down. Was glad to hear she has a roommate.

She mentioned she sometimes walks home from school alone, after dark. Set me off on a lecture. I explained that just because nice families live in a lot of the houses doesn't mean she's safe. This whole city is full of predators. I think she understands now why she sees so few people out after nightfall.

Should have a bad headache tonight but don't. Feeling pretty fine. Slowly I heal.


*Friday, January 3*
Mr. Goddard and I do five story in last two days, which seem to please him. Robert is ignoring us, like before. I wish I knew what is his problem. He doesn't seem to like Mr. Goddard, but for what reason? It is so silly. Today he ignore us by reading grad school catalogues at his desk. All the time he have one on his face: Stanford, Cal Berkeley, MIT.

After we finish, Mr. Goddard drive me home again. This is kind of him and better for me. I think it is not wise to walk in my neighborhood alone when it is dark. My teacher wait in his car until I go upstairs and check my apartment. If everything is O.K., I wave in window so he can leave. He suggest this smart idea.


*1/4/86*
In today's mail, a letter from our overstuffed Chair—

Dear John Goddard:

There appear to be two clerical errors on your 002 grade roster (IBM 39676). The CR (Credit) grades you recorded for students 553-5772 and 873-9634 are not in agreement with the results of the students' final exams.

Enclosed find a copy of the roster with the erroneous grades circled. Please see that these grades are corrected to

NC (No Credit) by Change of Grade Form TNES5/84 within one week.

Sincerely,

[The Watching Eye]

Letter is dated 12/31/85, which means Minter's giving me one day to comply. Generous of the man.

But you know, generous though you are, Herr Fartknock, I don't think I'm going to be able to meet your deadline. Not this one or any other. The very fact of your letter proves you're as impotent as a dildo in heat. The grades will stand.

Ball's in your court, bad ass.

*Sunday, January 5*

My teacher seems to have great sympathy for nature. In every story we input, he make me feel the time of year with his descriptions, help me imagine what it's like to live on farm in Kansas where land is flat and you can see forever. He describe thunderstorms, duststorms, fire on prairie and what the world look like on winter day when sun come up with only snow everywhere.

I feel the boy in the stories is lucky to grow up in such environment. If you live in touch with nature when you are little, it stay with you all your life, the peace and the feeling that man is just a small deal, everything consider.

Now I'm almost sure the stories are about my teacher. It's the same kid in every one and his kindly but strong personality remind me of Mr. Goddard. Who else it can be?

This evening I begin to read "The Good Earth," which my teacher let me pick from his bookcase when I return "Old Man and the Sea." Why did I choose "The Good Earth"? Because, on the cover is a little drawing of Chinese woman. That attract my curiosity. When Mr. Goddard tell me what the book is about, I decide to take it.

Do I like it? So far, yes. The characters are not beautiful or special. They are ordinary. But they interest me because they live back in the days when life was hard. I am curious about those days. Grandfather and grandmother use to tell about it.

I hope reading books will help my English, as teacher promise. Another way I will work to improve is by write in here, even though fall semester is over and I don't have to. Writing this journal has become my good habit so why quit?

What did I tell teacher about "Old Man and Sea"? I say I like it, good book.

*1/6/86*

At 3:00 P.M. today we were flying, about halfway through the second story of the afternoon, when the whole frigging system went down—taking with it about thirty minutes of unsaved edits.

We didn't come on-line again till nearly 5:00. Tina suggested we work late to make up the lost ground. Since Robert didn't show, there was no one to call us on it, but I was a little worried she might be breaking a rule. "Aren't you supposed to close?"

"Nobody tell me."

I went to the cafeteria, got some sandwiches, cookies and tea, and we worked till after 8:00, inputting three stories for the day— what I'd hoped for originally.

Tina's just great to work with. She's tireless, efficient, patient, always in a good mood. Because of her enthusiasm for the stories, I'm beginning to warm to them a little myself. Some aren't half bad, I guess, considering they were hatched by a pipsqueak.

The headache is heavy tonight. That bullshit with the computer was stressful. Dearly love sitting on my thumb, waiting.

*Monday, January 6*

Robert did not come to work today. He didn't even call. This is puzzling. Although he is strange person, he's always dependable till now. Will he come tomorrow? Who knows?

When I get home, in mailbox I find my grade report. I receive for Physics: B, Calc III: B, Symbolic Logic: A, and English 002: CR!

This is not good grade report, for me, but at least I pass English! Thanks to my teacher.

One of his stories I type today, I love it. He write it when he's only 17. "Face of the Enemy" it is call. It concern a boy who goes with his older cousins to hunt coyotes, which seem to be small wolf.

At first the boy is excited. He always admire his cousins and for many years he hear stories about what it is like to hunt coyotes. Now he is doing it.

He and his cousins join other men and they chase the coyotes in trucks, with radios to communicate. The boy see it is not hard to kill the animals in this way, shooting from the truck window. And when they stop to pick up the dead animals, the boy is surprise they are so small and skinny. He has heard many stories about coyotes killing cattle, but these are the size of dogs, and not fierce at all. To the boy, they look like dogs.

His cousins give him a gun so he can shoot, but he find he does not wish to kill any coyote. He aim his bullets behind them, hitting dirt only. He fails as coyote killer, disappoints his cousins, but inside he is glad.

The others kill eight coyotes, which the older men decide it is enough because it's getting dark. They hang the dead coyotes on a fence, upside down. The boy knows the bodies will stay there till they rot away. It is an insult to coyotes, and a warning.

He goes to one of the dead animals and finds the bullet hole. It is little hole, in the side, tight around his finger. He remembers how the bullet through that hole break the coyote's shoulders, rip his heart, end his life before he stop rolling on the grass.

The boy wanders if the stories about coyotes eating cows are true. It hasn't happen on their ranch, not in his life. He wonders why all the people he knows, good people, hate coyotes so much.

From this sad experience he learn important lesson I think. He learn you can't always go with the judgement of your family and friends. But there is more in the story than that.

*1/7/86*

We got a hell of a lot done today—necessary with only one night to go. For effort I was awarded the Mother of Migraines.

Back home I ran my symptoms past Dr. John and he put me temporarily on Writer's Turbo Cure. That is, Dilaudid and wine tonight to step on the headache, and Dilaudid with a little speed tomorrow morning for that good old sunrise motivation.

My headache (clamped in its narco-sarcophagus) is now but a faint throb. Sleep should come easy for Mr. Mellow.


*Thursday, January 9*

Last night I work with my teacher till midnight so we can finish the stories. We succeed, but when I come home I feel very tired, hungry too. I decide to eat a little soup before I go to bed. I put it on stove to heat, go in livingroom, sit on couch, take off shoes—that's all I remember. I fall asleep.

Next Rayneece is yelling "Wakeup, wakeup! Fire, fire!" I see big yellow flame in kitchen coming out of soup pan. Flame reach to the ceiling. Black smoke fill the apartment. Everywhere in the air dark greasy stuff float around and theres a very weird smell.

Rayneece turn off stove, put lid on pan to stop the flame. But still pan is burning inside. She push the lid down till fire go out. The smoke make her cough.

"Open the windows," she yell.

I run into our bedrooms, pull windows up. Then we both go downstairs on the lawn and watch smoke come out. Both of us are coughing.

"What was in that pan?" Rayneece say. I can tell she is not happy. I feel so stupid.

"Soup."

"Soup don't burn like that, girl."

Then I remember big plastic spoon I leave in the soup. When soup burn away, I guess the spoon melt and plastic catch fire. Plastic is petroleum base, so it burns hot, makes greasy ash. Now I know, but I never see it before.

I apologize for my carelessness, thank Rayneece for waking me, because by myself I don't think I will wake up in time. Maybe she save my life.

But my apology does not satisfy her. "Why didn't the smoke alarm go off?" she demand. "Did you unhook the wire when you clean?"

"No."

"You probably sucked it off with the vacuum."

I refuse to answer. She can accuse all she want. I didn't suck anything but dust.

"We'll have to repaint the whole place," she say. "You know that, don't you?"

Finally I lose my temper. "I burn the apartment," I tell her, "so I will paint it. You don't have to do anything but say what color. But in future, when your friends come over and throw up on bathroom floor, spill beer on carpet, you clean up. Not me."

Even in the dark I see her smiling. "What happen to little miss polite?" she ask.

"Lose her patience."

"Good. Your talking straight for once. Usually you so busy being polite I can't tell what you think."

I can see her point when she say that, in a way. Rayneece herself is very direct. She always tell you exactly what she think, and if you don't want to know, better not ask. I guess to a person like her, someone like me who dislike to be blunt and rude seem dishonest. Maybe I am dishonest, but it is how I was taught. With my people, to be direct like Rayneece is bad manners.

When smoke is gone, we go inside. I offer her tea and for once she accept. I offer almond cookies too. We sit at kitchen table, drink tea, eat cookies and talk, try to ignore black ceiling and awful smell.

I learn she come back early because she fight with her mother over her mother's new boyfriend. He is only 24. She say her mom has have many boyfriends, ever since Rayneece's dad die in Germany in a car wreck in 1971, when she is only six. Her dad was soldier in the Army, and because of that Rayneece gets money from the government until age 21. That's why she doesn't have to work. It's not because she's rich, like I think.

I have not seen Robert, and he hasn't call. He miss every day this week. This is inexcusable, but I will not tell the Director of Work Study, for now.

How do I know, maybe Robert leave the city in a hurry for family emergency. Or maybe he is injured, unable to call. I will protect him as long as I can. Probably I will wait till classes start next week. Then lab will get busy again. If he's still gone, I must tell Director or maybe lose my job.


1/9/86

We finished inputting the collection last night. Early this morning I got it off by express mail.

We really had to push these last three days. When I pay Tina I'm going to add a bonus. Impossible, though, to repay with money dedication like hers. She was so tired last night when I dropped her off she could barely keep her eyes open.

I guess it's predictable that my work on the collection has brought back old memories. Tonight it's Penokee on my mind. I can still see every detail of the place. The unpaved main street—with no name that I know—oiled in summer to keep the dust down. The big old elm trees. Its four houses and feed store. And McCune's, the town's recreation and entertainment center, compressed into a one-floor white cinderblock structure with a small picture window facing the streeet. There was a sandwich shop in front and in back a pool room just large enough for its lone bumper pool table.

The last time I was in McCune's I was with Garner Scarbrough. We were playing French pool and sipping cokes spiked with bourbon. That was the night we got the bright idea to drive to Denver and talk to the Army recruiters.

Garner played safety on our football team and was one crazy sonofabitch. He only weighed about 145, but he was very fast and hit like a kamikazi on every play. He loved to tackle with his head.

He also loved to run through fallen bodies stomping indiscriminately on exposed hands. By our senior year, almost every player in the league was gunning for him, including half our team.

Anyhow, you figure it, but this is the guy I pick to drive drunk with, in the middle of the night, all the way to the Rocky Mountains. And why? To sign away my ass so Uncle Sam can ship me off to a war I don't believe in.

Actually, enlistment was something we'd both been kicking around. Garner because he never intended to go to college and figured the draft would get him anyway. Me because with all my naive philosophizing I'd concluded that college was a cop out, a safety chute reserved for rich boys. I'd made up my mind to face the draft and let it take me and that's probably what I would've done if Garner and I hadn't gotten drunk together that night.

I asked for assignment to the Medical Corps because I didn't want to kill (nor did I personally feel at war with the Vietnamese). They granted my request. I became an Army medic.

It seemed to me so simple and logical at the time, though now, looking back, I think I must have been under some kind of Hemingway spell—in my life as in my prose style. Didn't Hemingway work as an ambulance driver in WWI? And wasn't he, in his heart of hearts, defying death in order to gather experiences to write about, as I no doubt was?

My decision did not appear so brilliant after I sobered up, returned home, and informed my family. I thought at least Dad would understand, because of his own war service. I'll never forget the look on his face when I told him. Disappointment and worry etched themselves into his every feature as he tried to find something encouraging to say, but couldn't. Mom broke down and cried, they tell me. My brother thought I'd gone nuts.

They were all three right, of course, as I learned too late and far too well over the next 24 months.

*Saturday, January 11*
Yesterday, Rayneece and me go to store and choose new paint for our apartment: sky blue semigloss for kitchen, eggshell for living room. I choose white for my bedroom because I always want as much light as I can get. Rayneece choose black for her room because she say it helps her sleep.

Last night we take turns standing on ladder to scrub greasy kitchen ceiling. Today we paint the whole apartment. With two people it is easy, after Rayneece show me how to use the roller.

We open our windows to dry the paint, and they are still open. Now it is 7:00 pm and I am freezing. I wear jeans, one shirt, two sweaters, two pairs of socks, and my mittens, therefore its hard to write.

Rayneece tell me her grades for fall are one A, three B's, one C. That makes 3.0 grade average—exactly what she needs to keep her scholarship. I guess she knows what she's doing. Probably top grades are not important in her major.


*1/12/86*
Stayed on the Dilaudid through the weekend to bonk the headache and tried to max out on rest. Saturday night I found an all-Beethoven marathon on FM and for the next twenty hours cruised to the Ubermusic, drifting in and out of sleep.

Now it's late Sunday night, Beethoven's over, and I've used up the Dilaudid (which is probably good, unless the headache revisits).

Tomorrow and Tuesday are registration. Means I still have time to do spring lesson plans and syllabi. Some more good sleep tonight, maybe, to set me up.

Christ those stories tuckered me out.


*Monday, January 13*
Something strange occur as I register for English 101 today. When I ask the lady to give me IBM card for Mr. Goddard's class, she ask to see my schedule. I assume she must check if I have that time

open. However, I watch her and what she do is turn my schedule over to read where my name is. Then she tell me Mr. Goddard's class is fill, even though I can see cards for his class in her box.

I ask about the cards.

"Those are reserve for English Majors," she say with fake smile. "Are you English Major?"

I admit no.

"Here," she say, and hand me card for 101 class at same time, one with professor Braeme. Naturally, the class fits my schedule. I don't really want it, because I don't trust this lady, but I can't think of good reason to give it back.

Walking home from gym I feel so scared and the feeling won't go away. It seem to me the lady plan to keep me out of Mr. Goddard's class before she ever see me. Did she also plan to give me this teacher Braeme? If she did, it can be bad. Braeme might fail me.

Maybe Mr. Goddard should know about this. Maybe he is familiar with Braeme and can tell me is Braeme a good teacher, or a bad teacher, and is he fair?


*1/14/86*

When I dropped by the computer lab today to give Tina her check, she informed me a flat-chested woman with dyed red hair and a phony smile kept her out of my 101 class at registration yesterday.

The Hump? I asked some questions to make sure. It was the glasses that did it. No one else in the Department wears such over-size lenses.

But why would Humper do registration? All the tenured faculty, her included, shuffle off the penny-ante shit on their subordinates. Did she have an ulterior motive? Hey, do vampires suck blood?

My 101 wasn't closed yesterday—that's for damn sure. There were still two seats open this afternoon because I called and checked right after talking to Tina. There's no policy to reserve spaces for English majors either. That's total B.S.

It does look like a set-up, but one part doesn't compute. I can't picture Dan Braeme going along with some shady plot to trap a student. He's always been straight with me, and from everything I've heard about him he's an excellent teacher.

I suggested to Tina that she hold tight for now, see how things go in his class, and if necessary drop before the deadline. My feeling is she'll prove herself with her writing, just as she did with me last semester.

Not wise to raise a big stink right now, demand they put her in my class. Might look bad under the circumstances. Also, if we can get Dan Braeme behind Tina, then she's got it made. He's respected by everyone in the Department. He'd put the tenured professor's seal of approval on her.

I'll bet the Hump believes Tina can't write on her own (without Coach Goddard). She assumes that a fair but demanding teacher like Braeme will expose the fraud. I'd say she's in for a surprise.

*Thursday, January 16*
For Calculus IV I have Dr. Kim again. I think he's a little disappoint in me for making B in his class last semester. He knows I can do better. I will try to prove he's right.

For Computer Science 201, Dr. Parviz. His syllabus is 4 pages long, very much work if we do it all. From the way he talk, I think he will be difficult. He is the kind of teacher you better try hard or you will be in big trouble. I usually do O.K. with teachers like that, if they are fair.

For Matrix Theory, Dr. Singh. I do not take him before, but other students say he's good. Today he make excellent impression. He seem the kind of teacher who challenge you, but still he wants everyone to do well. He explain so clear, have good sense of humor, tell us please ask questions. His class I can enjoy maybe, and learn too.

For English 101, Professor Braeme of course. Our first class he lecture us the whole time. His subject is John Swift, a writer. I did not understand much, but I did learn Swift write "Gulliver Travels." It concern a trip John Swift take in his boat to different countries.

Sometimes Professor Braeme stop talking to ask question, and

all the others in class are dumb like me, nobody know the answer—
except one student. His name is Alexander. He is tall and has red
hair and little brown spots all over his face. Obviously he read
"Gulliver Travels" before.

For next time, Braeme assign us another story by John Swift
call "A Modest Proposal." I start it, but I only read three page because what John write in there is so disgusting. He say we should
cook and eat Irish babies, and how they taste so good, and how we
will save money by treat them like little animals we raise for food.

I don't know why somebody would write such awful, sick ideas,
and I don't know why Dr. Braeme assign. However, I will try to
finish tomorrow. It is the assignment.

My first impression of Professor Braeme is not good. But I remind myself that I can not judge any person so soon. I must wait
and see.

Mr. Goddard insist on pay me $525 for typing his stories. I did
not argue. I accept his check, act surprise at the amount (I was), put
it in my purse and take home.

When I pray at shrine tonight, I burn the check and make this
prayer—that I pass English 101. I know Mr. Goddard would not
like what I did, but since the money is mine, I can spend it how I
want. To me, if the prayer works, the money is worth it. Besides,
how can I take money from a teacher that help me so much?

*1/16/86*
Waiting in my campus mailbox this morning was Minter's latest sal-
vo in the grade change wars.

> Greetings:
>     You were instructed by our letter of 12/31/85 to change
> two erroneous course grades. You have not done so. As a
> result of your delinquency in this matter, the students in-
> volved are under the false impression they passed your
> class, and both have enrolled in 101 sections for which they
> should not be eligible.

When these students learn the true state of their affairs, they may feel acute disappointment and anger. They may feel they have been made to pay for your intemperate behavior. They may wish to file a grievance against you for the confusion caused them in their academic careers, and we believe they would be within their rights to do so.

We are enclosing two change of grade forms for your convenience. They are complete except for your signature. Sign them and return them to the Department with all possible dispatch.

Your failure to comply with this directive immediately will constitute a serious breach of English Department governance.

With concern,
[Fearless Leader]

So, the level of impotent bluster is ballooning, is it? How scary. I'm about to breach a governance.


*Friday, January 17*
Director of Work Study call today, ask for Robert. I think uh-oh, now he's going to get caught. But I realize if she call him, she must not know. So I tell her he miss today—which is truth, but only small part of truth. She leave message for him to turn in the 1032's.

I look everywhere and I cant find such forms in the cabinets or in Robert's desk. They may be in the files but the files are lock and Robert has the key.

I really don't know why I didn't tell her Robert doesn't come to work anymore. I must tell her very soon. Until then, I keep running lab by myself, hope he come back.

Unfortunately the lab is not working correctly now that the semester start. When I go to class, I put BACK SOON sign on the door. Sometimes when I return, people are waiting. They know we're suppose to be open all day. I'm lucky nobody complain.

*1/18/86*

Got the cast off today and turned in the cane. The ankle feels pretty good, but it's weak from disuse and tires when I walk any distance.

The rest of me is in decent shape, mainly from lugging the damn cast. Climbing the steps to campus from C lot every day has been a workout. Certainly haven't gotten fat. My wind has suffered though. It's back about where it was before I started running. Square two. But if the headaches improve, I could be running again in a few weeks.

I'm off all drugs—including wine and grass—for at least a few days. Clean out the old system. Drugs are always questionable, a necessary evil at best. They all have the tendency to boomerang.

The only perfect drug I've heard of is the one Helen mixed into the wine she served Telemachus when he visited, a tonic with the power to annul grief and erase all painful memories. The stuff was so efficient, Homer tells us, that after taking it you could watch, without a tear, your parents or siblings being hewn to bits with a sword. No mention of negative side effects. Duration of stone: hours apparently.

Well, I could go for some of that. Who couldn't? I'm sure modern medicine is searching for an equivalent. It must be the holy grail of current drug research. Think of the bucks, think of the bucks!


*Saturday, January 18*

I find Robert's home address on envelope in his desk, look on map to see where it is. Not far away. It's on the other side of freeway, but there are streets where I can cross.

This afternoon I ride there on my bike, get lost once, but finally find it. I meet Robert's mother, who cannot speak English, and his little brother Luis who is 8. Luis explain Robert work on a house nearby, and I can see him if I want.

I take Luis on back of my bike so he can show me where to go. On the way he ask, "Are you Robert's girlfriend?"

"We work together."

"Oh."

Then he tell me I'm pretty.

"You just saying it," I kid him.

"No I'm not." He make a frown, kind of mad.

I find I like this serious little guy. In some way, he seem more growed up than his big brother who is over twice his age. He take me to a yellow house with bare black roof. Robert is up there, hitting nails with a hammer. He see me, but do you think he come down politely to speak to me? Of course not. He answer my questions while he hit the nails.

Sometimes I can't hear him, but I do hear he's quitting school. He didn't register for spring classes. School is for nerds, he tell me.

His attitude bother me. Did I ride all these trencherous miles, with cars blowing horns at me and tough guys whistle, just to hear school is for nerds?

In my anger I say what I think. "Just because you get low GRE's, that's no reason to be a crybaby."

He come down the roof and ladder so fast I think he's going to hit me. I look for my bicycle but I see Luis is riding it many houses away.

Robert approach me with something on his hand. It's his billfold. He take out paper and give to me. The paper is from Educational Testing Service: his GRE scores. Actually, he did very well. In numerical, top 1%. In physics, top 2%. Verbal, top 50%—not bad for science student, I think.

"So why you drop out?" I ask.

At first he won't tell me, but I keep bug him till he admit he did a dumb thing. He wait till last fall, his senior year, to take English 002. Then he fail the final. He was in cafeteria with me, flunking his test while I flunk mine, although I never see him.

Now he say there is no way for him to finish his English requirement before graduation, therefore he can't graduate. Since he can't graduate, he can't go to grad school next year. So what's the use?

As we discuss, I see he is bitter about what happen. It seem to me his real problem is he's afraid to take English 002 again. Probably because he fear to fail.

"Who was your teacher?" I ask.

"I don't know," he say. "Franklin."

Franklin—that silly man who substitute for Mr. Goddard. "You fail because you have bad teacher. With good teacher you can pass."

He don't believe me that there are good English teachers. He hate them all.

I ignore his negative attitude and tell what it's like in Mr. Goddard's class. I explain the papers we write, how we work in groups to build arguments, our grammars lessons, and Mr. Goddard's helping comments. All these make you get better for sure, I say.

"I'd never take his class," he say.

"Why?"

"He's in love with himself."

I don't think it's true. And Robert won't tell me why he think that.

Finally he did listen, though. He admit he can graduate in time if he pass 002 this spring and English 101 in summer. But he say he must consider if he want to enroll in Mr. Goddard's class. I think maybe he will do it, if Mr. Goddard ask him.

Now I must speak to my teacher, find out can he tolerate Robert as his student. I do not look forward. I know Mr. Goddard doesn't like Robert. Why should he? Has Robert ever treated him better than dirt?


*1/19/86*

Tina Le phoned this afternoon and although I'm not quite sure how, she talked me into enrolling Robert (her surly supervisor) in my already overenrolled 002 class. No, it's even worse. I've agreed to go to his house and solicit him to enroll in my overenrolled class, because apparently he's too proud to come to me, humiliated by his failure in 002 last fall.

Well, Tina did save my butt by helping me with those stories. And although I have little personal use for the Prince of Pout, I definitely sympathize with his generic situation. Looks like another talented student being humped out of school by an English Department gone bonkers.

Tina says he's majoring in physics and has a 3.9 GPA. Did well on his GREs. Speaks English fluently, according to her. Since he's never spoken to me, I wouldn't know, so I was glad she could fill me in.


*Sunday, January 19*

Mr. Goddard pick me up this afternoon and we go to Robert's. When we arrive, Robert is fixing car with his father in garage. Because Robert's head is stuck inside the motor, Mr. Goddard must talk to his behind.

My teacher ignore this and tell Robert about the English Department's writing courses. He explain why they are not fair—how so many students fail every semester in all the classes, even very good writers. He say last fall many more fail 002 than pass.

Although everybody on campus knows this stuff, to Robert it is new. But now that he knows, he is angry. He pull his head out of the motor to ask questions. Why do the English teachers want to fail so many students? Why does the University let it happen? And so on. My teacher answer each one politely, the bestest he can.

Soon the sky is getting dark and Luis come out to ask if we will stay for dinner. His Mom is fixing it. How can we say no?

At the table, Mr. Goddard fortunately speak a little Spanish and Mr. Acuna speak a little English—so the men can talk together while they eat and drink beer.

Robert has the sweetest sisters, Cecelia age 16, and Lupe age 14. They are eager girls with big smiles, I like them right away. They ask me a million questions about Cal State. They want to go there when they are old enough. Robert is first in their family to enter college, and they both decide to follow his footsteps. He has not tell them he drop out—so I don't mention.

On the way home, Mr. Goddard say he believe Robert won't take his class. One chance in four, he estimate.

"We tried, all we can do."

My teacher is patient man, as I observe tonight. He handle Robert just right. By the time we leave Robert is smiling at Mr. Goddard with his teeth. That proves something. I think one chance in two.

*1/20/86*

Somewhat to my surprise, Robert showed for class today and behaved quite well. After class I signed his add form. So he's in.

He wants to be called Roberto now, the name his parents gave him. Raises the questions of when and why he became Robert. Now that he seems to be changing back, is the metamorphosis complete?

I would guess his current identity crisis is courtesy of the English Department. If so, good thing. Best for him to know that for some in our society just his last name, or his accent, or his brown skin will always be enough to brand him persona non grata, a smudge of protoplasm begging to be stared through on virtually all occasions.

The reversion bodes well for Roberto's future. Maybe, in time, he'll be able to lighten the chip on his shoulder.

*Tuesday, January 21*

Dr. Braeme lecture us about "Modest Proposal" for most of class. I did not understand all of it, but some things he say help me, I think. He explain John Swift wasn't talking about real babies, but only makeup ones, satires. The satires represent how the English mistreat the Irish back in those days—by take their land, tax them till they starve, kill them too, sometimes, if they try and fight back.

Here is the important thing. John Swift write the story to make the English people ashame, so they will stop being mean to the Irish. The reason that's important is because of our assignment. We are suppose to write essay in class next Tuesday on whether John Swift make effective arguments in his story.

To me, the assignment is not difficult. I think John's arguments are not effective, and here's why:

First, his satire of eating the babies is too ugly and depressing to work as effective argument. Naturally it gets your attention, but it is such a sick idea that you must dislike and distrust the person who think it: John Swift. If he wants to argue that the English mistreat the Irish, he must do it in more calm and logical manner.

Second, the way John tell his story, everybody in it looks bad—the English, the Irish, even John. And that's not effective either. Instead of discussing the Irish like all are animals and beggars and thieves, he should show their sympathetic side, and certainly he should respect them as humans. If they are really like animals, as he show in the story, why shouldn't the English treat them as animals?

Finally, I do not believe "Modest Proposal" persuade the English to leave the Irish alone. The English Army are they not still in Ireland? And why do the Irish blow up all those bombs—to celebrate how free and happy they are?

Mr. Goddard tell us good persuasive writing must change your mind on an issue. In my opinion, John Swift's story isn't going to change many people's mind. His methods are too immature, too dramatic, too sick.

My position is quite definite, but one thing worry me a little. I think Dr. Braeme like "Modest Proposal." If I argue my way, I can go against what he belief, and will he like that? Then I remember what Mr. Goddard advice us to do in such situation. Argue what you belief, he say, because you will argue more strong.

At work, Robert keeps correcting me because I mispronounce his name. Since yesterday, he insists I say Roberto, but I can't always remember.

At first I think it's his way to tell me we are friends now, because he wants me to call him by his real name. However, I find out different when he correct one of the grad students exactly the way he correct me. He makes everybody call him Roberto. I'm not sure why.

*1/23/86*

Eva's no longer my editor. Don't know what happened, but she's definitely gone because the new guy—Kratzer—called today to say he'd be on board till publication. No explanations.

He liked most of my changes. But he wants Alan Crossbee to narrate *all* the stories. We had an argument, though not a big one. Probably I just opposed him on principle; it's bloody fucking annoying having to change horses in midstream. His idea is not bad in itself.

Eva had the same idea and I talked her out of it. That's because one story would have to be dropped. But it's a weaker one—I could live without it. And of the others only three or four would require much rewriting. Certainly a common narrator would lend more unity.

He's giving me three weeks. Should be enough. The headaches are almost gone so I can work long hours.

*Friday, January 24*

Tonight I read "The Good Earth" till I come to the end. The story interest me because O-Lan and her husband Wang Lung struggle against so many problems, but work hard, survive, raise family and become rich. It is amazing the things that happen to them.

The end is sad but I like it. Wang Lung and his wife have spoil their kids. And the author suggest that when Wang Lung die, his children will spend away all his wealth with their wasteful, foolish behaviors. In time all the land and money will be gone, and Wang Lung's grandchildren will be poor people just like he and his wife begin.

It is awful how Wang Lung treat O-Lan once he become rich. He chase women of low character and leave his wife to suffer. In my opinion, O-Lan die of sadness. I would not want to be woman in China in those days. You must either be obedient wife and endure husband's cruelties, or a slave, kind of prostitute, owned by some wealthy man or family. For single woman life was quite tragic.

Maybe it is better for women in China today, but I don't want to be communist either! I had have enough of that already.

*1/27/86*

Minter saw me in the hall this morning and asked me into his office. Humper was already there, seated, ready for trouble. For once in his useless life, our chairman came to the point. He asked if I was going to change the grades.

I refused.

He asked why.

I told him both students did passing work in the course.

He pointed out they failed their finals.

I said I averaged in their failing finals, and they passed—overall.

He said you can't do that.

I said I did it.

He turned to the Hump. "Do you have any questions for him?"

"No," she said quietly, face stern, mouth drawn. Clearly, I'd been a naughty, naughty boy.

He told me I could go.

Screw 'em. What can they do?

At the very worst, they can take my job—no gem. But they don't have the guts to try. I'm pretty sure.

More probably, they'll each put a negative letter in my job file. To chicken-livered academics like themselves, a critical letter is tantamount to being gutted. They shake and shiver at the prospect. Thus they expect me to shake and shiver.

Let the letters flow, knuckleheads. I want full documentation. Let's light up this precedent for all to see.


*Thursday, January 28*

Today Dr. Braeme hand out essay call "The New Narcissists." The author argue American young people are selfish, greedy, materialistic. He say they don't have any values except me, me, me. As I listen to Dr. Braeme read, I can tell he like what the author say. His voice become big and he smile sometimes, like he approve. When he finish, he ask what do we think?

Alexander rise his hand and agree with author. Its just like this girl who go to his high school. She is a very spoilt one, whose parents buy her all she ask: Mercedes car, mechanical ski slope, plastic surgery on her chin and nose. And because she have all these things, she believe she's better than others.

One night she get drunk on cocaine and run over two little kids in crosswalk, kill them. According to Alexander, she don't care because she know her lawyers will keep her out of jail. And that's what happen. Alexander say everyone in his high school still look up to her, just because she is rich. Everyone wants to be her friend.

Dr. Braeme turn to rest of us and ask what do we think. Is author right or not? But nobody have nothing to say. So our teacher and Alexander do all the talking. No problem, they are used to it.

Actually, I agree with this author, in a way. To me, he is right that American young people are selfish and materialistic. But I think he make error in logic. He neglect to consider that American capitalist society is base on selfishness and materialism. It's not just kids who are selfish, so are their parents and everyone else. So why criticize young people and pretend they are the only ones?

I didn't say these things in class because I'm not sure Dr. Braeme want to hear them. And I won't start my paper now. It is not due till one week. Maybe next class Braeme will return our essays on "Modest Proposal." Then I can see how he grade before I begin new assignment.


*1/29/86*

Roberto got NC+ on his first essay—partly because he added late, but mainly because of unclear sentences. The guy shoots for an elevated baroque style on the order of Martin Luther King's, but he's not up to it yet. The result, frequently, is turgid murk.

When I gave his paper back in class he was definitely not happy with the grade. He sat brooding for about ten minutes, then rose and stalked out.

Not a good sign, but I'm hoping he may cool down by next class. Let him think it over. Let him check out some of those bejeweled sentences he no doubt treasures. If he's got an honest bone in his body, he's going to see some of those jewels turn to gooseberries over the next few days.

The ankle is back, pretty much. I've been walking in the neighborhood nearly every day, adding distance, pace. This evening I did about four miles in an hour and twenty minutes.

Soon I'll be running.

*Thursday, January 30*

Rayneece has a new man. His name is Kenneth and I think he's Korean. He's tall, good-looking, but he seems a little conceited. He always wear a suit even though he is a student.

I guess I should not expect Rayneece to change her ways. She take a little vacation from guys, that's all, and now vacation over. If you like guys as much as she does, I suppose it's certain you will find a new one pretty soon, when you have time.

Dr. Braeme give our "Modest Proposal" papers back. My grade is C–. He didn't seem to like what I say, and in many places he write comments to tell me why I'm wrong. For example, where I call the author John, he write "Are you a personal friend of Swift? If not, please refer to him as Swift. Notice too that his first name is *not* John." A lot of the comments are like that.

He also circle all the places where I say "story," and write in margin that I need to learn difference between "story" and "essay." But he does not explain the difference.

My main mistake is I do not understand the persona Swift use in his story. Dr. Braeme explain my arguments are not relevant because they apply to the persona in the essay, not to author, John Swift.

Well he's right, I'm sure. Because I do not even know what persona is. I look in dictionary and it say persona mean "a person," or else "characters in a drama." But these definitions do not help me much. I can't see how they relate to Swift's essay.

I'd like to find out exactly what I did wrong so I won't repeat. However, I find I do not want to ask Dr. Braeme to explain. Usually I don't understand him, anyway.

Maybe Mr. Goddard can help.

*1/30/86*

Tina Le came in during office hours to show me her first paper for Braeme's class. It's a rhetorical analysis of "A Modest Proposal" and she got a C–. If we leave the wisdom of the assignment aside, the grade is maybe about right, because some of her arguments were not the strongest.

What surprised me is that old Dan's marginal commentary is all in the attack mode. He points out every damn thing she did wrong without a word about what she did right. Acts as though she had zero good arguments, which was hardly the case. Not the strategy I'd pick if I wanted to help her write better.

For the next assignment he's had them read Roper's "The New Narcissists." It was used for the 101 final about a year ago. Most of my students found it trivial and annoying on account of Roper's narrow point of view. However, the pass rate on that final was relatively high. I'm sure it's because Roper invites successful counterarguments with his frequently exposed fanny. It's like he's got a target painted there and the students loved nailing it.

Tina sees the target, and she's got a quiver of arrows straight and true, but she's worried because she thinks Braeme supports Roper's position and might grade her down for taking the other side.

I hope I did the right thing. I told her to argue what she believes. Even if Danny boy isn't quite the teacher I thought, surely he's got enough intellectual honesty to recognize and reward good arguments, whatever position they defend. Ultimately, it doesn't really matter how snippy he is in his comments, as long as he grades fair.

*Saturday, February 1*

Rayneece stay here with Ken last night. He is her loudest boyfriend so far, louder even than Rayneece. In his mind I think he see it as competition, and he will win.

This morning, while I wash dishes, he come out in his suit, but no shoes, and try to sell me water filter for sink. He claim the city water has poisons in it, killing people little by little every day. But with the water filter poisons get clean out and the water becomes pure like rain.

I tell him I can't afford.

"Only 42 cents a day," he say. "You can't afford 42 cents to protect your body from hazardous chemicals?"

"No."

He look concern. "Your health is your most precious possession. It's not worth 42 cents?"

"No."

When he see for sure I will not buy, he give up, start bragging about he is such good salesman, has 6 people working for him, will be millionaire by age 30. Do I have a boyfriend, he ask? I finish dishes, leave them in drainer to dry, go in my room and shut door so he will leave me alone.

I do not trust that guy. He is insincere in my opinion. Of all Rayneece's men, this one is less likable to me.


2/2/86

Another strange dream last night.

I was at a dance club in some border town—Tijuana, Mexicali maybe. Across the room from me a stunning woman. Through the hanging smoke she's giving me the eye.

I ask her for a dance. Up close, she's even more beautiful— hair blacker than a moonless night, eyes sky blue, slender shapely body.

The music is slow and romantic. We dance close, so close our thighs touch and her chest is against me, soft and heavy. She sighs against my neck and the cool smell of old roses envelops me. Under the roses I can detect a much fainter odor, less pleasant. As I try to place it, it increases, thickens, becomes heavy in my head, dizzying. The stench of rotting flesh.

Terrified, I try to push her away, but she clings more tightly, begins to lead, moving to the music with ferocious strength. I'm pulled along like a rag doll, twisting and wrenching every muscle to get her off me, but I can't. She crushes my torso with her steel arms until I begin to suffocate, wind whistling through my lips.

I look into her eyes again. The sockets are empty. Of anything. Bottomless. It's like looking through two knotholes into the reaches of infinite space.

End of dream.

Never had one like that before. Don't want to have it again.


*Monday, February 3*

When I consider my math and science teachers, there are some I like as people, and some I don't like so much. This semester for example, I like best Dr. Singh, my Matrix Theory teacher. He is intelligent man, but not arrogant. He try hard to help you understand, and he won't put you down for being wrong. Also he is the same with every student.

In the other hand, there is my Computer Science teacher, Professor Parviz, not a friendly type. He is cold person. His face is like a rock, and sometimes he ignore our questions. But at least he doesn't have favorites. He treat everybody bad.

In between, there's Dr. Kim, my Calculus teacher, who is quite fair person and will help if you have a problem in his class. But when he gets behind in his lecture and has to hurry, then he will get impatient. I feel he is kind person but with strict personality that will not bend.

My math and science teachers each have different character, but one thing I like about them all. When they give assignment, they explain exactly what they want. That way, if you work hard, you can be sure to succeed—because the correct path is known.

My main complaint on many English teachers is I can't understand their assignments, or else they want me to say certain things in my paper but I don't know what they want. Because of these confusions, I can study English hard, yet fall on my face.

Often English does not seem fair to me, which is why I hate it (sometimes).

*2/4/86*

Since Roberto walked out of class the other day, his attendance has been regular and his behavior human. He acts cordial to me, but very on the surface, formal. I think he's trying to show respect, but without any hint of kowtowing to the man.

That's his classroom behavior. Today, when I went in the computer lab to work on the stories, I witnessed what I take to be his "my turf" behavior. He ignored me completely, just as before.

Tina came to work later and offered to help me, but I told her it really wasn't necessary. I'm almost well now and she has her own work to do.

An hour later as I was trying to save edits I hit some sequence of keys that turned my whole document into a Martian dialect. To my embarrassment, I had to ask Tina for help after all. It took her just a few keystrokes to rectify my goof, saving me more work than I want to think about.


*Wednesday, February 5*

I come home from school and find this strange object attach to kitchen sink. I realize it must be the wonderful water filter.

Well, a rich man can afford to give such things to his girl friend, I'm thinking. I turn on the faucet and fill a glass. The water is slower than before, but clearer. And the taste is better, it's true. It doesn't taste like chemicals.

When Rayneece come home, I learn the filter is not a gift. Ken sell to her for 55 cents a day.

"He tell me 42 cents."

"That's for the two year filter," she say, "but I buy the three year."

"And how many days you pay 55 cents?"

She don't know.

Well, sounds sad to me, because I think he's cheating her, but I don't say nothing. She wants to believe Ken is one fantastic guy who love her truly and would never cheat. If I point to negatives, she will probably think I'm jealous.

*2/5/86*

I was wrong. Minter and the Hump *are* going for my job. Couldn't be more blatant. I got my annual evaluation from the Promotion and Retention Committee today and they've lowered my ranking from 1 (excellent) to 4 (poor). Means I won't be offered classes next year. In effect, I've been fired.

Three reasons are given for the new ranking, all under the heading Professional Conduct:

1) "insubordinate"

2) "over-identifies with his students, leading to inappropriate fraternization"

3) "behaves in an abusive manner toward colleagues"

Oddly, there is virtually no other information on my evaluation form. Nothing about my publications, nothing about the students' evaluations of me, no mention of lesson plans or assignments. In past years I've been highly commended in all those areas. And the areas carry much weight in the overall ranking. Why nothing this year?

Even the timing is strange. We usually get our job evals in April. I went back to the mailroom and checked. Nobody else got one.

It's clear I'm being railroaded, and in a crude, heavy-handed way. I'd have expected them to be more circumspect, to wipe their prints, especially when firing someone so qualified. Is it the arrogance of power—shark stupid? Certainly Fearless Leader and MHP are not the brightest bulbs. I guess it's possible.

Or maybe it's a setup. Maybe they expect me to fly off the handle and create a big scene—providing further evidence of collegial molestation.

Or maybe they know something I don't.


*Thursday, February 6*

Professor Braeme assign story for our next paper. I read it tonight to see will it be hard. Surprise! I like it a lot.

Author is same who write book about old man and fish, Hemingway. The new story have old man in it too, but this one live in city and is alcoholic. The title is "A Clean, Well-Lighted Place." It seem to refer to cafe where the old man drinks, and to similar places where people try to forget their lonely feelings. I believe the story concern all persons who are lonely.

The old man miss his wife who die. He like to sit outside the cafe at night so he can watch the shadows the trees make and feel how quiet is the street when all the cars and people go home. He is deaf, but he can sense the quiet. He finds comfort in such things. He like to drink brandy too, and I think he like ordering waiters—do this do that.

To me it is excellent story, complex, very sad and true. I can write good paper maybe, but of course that depend on question Dr. Braeme ask.

2/7/86

Visited the Office of the Dean of Academic Affairs to find out about grievances. The Dean's secretary, a bit of a fussbudget, waxed helpful once she understood my predicament. Think she sympathized.

My case does provide sufficient grounds for grievance, according to her. Most matters grieved are much smaller than mine. Why put it off, I decided. The paperwork was a snap. Took five minutes. The hearing will happen within sixty days.

I asked who'd be representing the English Department.

"A member of the University's legal staff."

"A lawyer."

"Yes."

"Should I hire a lawyer?"

She explained carefully why she couldn't advise me in such matters, then added, "Personally, I would."

She's right, I think. After all, I'm taking on not just Minter and the Hump, but the whole frigging CSU. Hadn't quite dawned on me till this afternoon. The university administration will want to win this thing merely to preserve their power over people in my position. If I don't have a lawyer, I'll be fighting them with a pea shooter.

So. Hire a lawyer. Shit.

*Sunday, February 9*

Tet begins today in Vietnam. I had plan to celebrate in small ways, by myself. Then Rayneece see me cut fruit for offering and ask what I'm doing.

When I explain, she say my little celebration isn't enough. "It's your New Year. You got to do it right." She want to celebrate with me, and I think great. Usually she is too busy for stuff like that.

We go to Vietnamese grocery in Monterey Park and buy Tet foods. I pick ones I think we both can like: steam chicken, spring rolls, pork paté, sticky rice with boil fish, spicy salad. Then we take home and eat. She seem to enjoy most of them. But I notice she did not eat much fishes.

Later she drink tea with me and we talk. I learn she and Ken have big fight yesterday and break up. It happen as they come back from Palm Springs. Ken feel she flirt with this man in hotel and they argue about it. Ken blow his top and make her get out of car in desert. Then he drive away. She must beg a ride from some guy she dont know.

I tell her losing Ken is not so bad. She deserve a better one.

She just shrug. She feel kind of depress about her relationships right now. She worry will she go through life with many men one after another, like her mom. That bothers her a lot. She can see her mom isn't happy.

I tell her she doesn't have to be like her mom. Just be patient, wait for a good guy to come along. When she find him, stick with that guy. She can do it if she wants.

She think I don't understand. "You hardly notice men," she say. "If a man will be interest in you, you probably wouldn't even know. But I notice guys. And guys notice me. Been that way since I was a little girl. Hard for me to stay with one forever. You know what they say. Lots of fish in the sea."

Unfortunately, she thinks she's helpless. When she falls in love, she falls, nothing she can do—accordingly to her. At that point, I find it hard to have sympathy. I must wander: how can it be love if she feel it for so many guys? Deep inside, I think maybe she want to be like her mother.

Later, she tell me about her mom's boyfriend who rape her when she is 15. He did it for the whole summer, until the police arrest him for something else, put him in jail. I imagine how it will be, live in same house with man who rape you. To see him every day, look in his eyes, know you can't get away. Unless you run away from home.

It's not so different from what happen to me. Because of her experience, I feel she can probably understand. So I tell her a little about when that man keep me in cave on island. She is quite sweet. She give me big hug, say what happen to me is much worst than what happen to her. Maybe she's right, I don't know. Both seem bad to me.

Strangely, she don't blame her mom's friend. She believe she tempt that man, so he can't help himself. She don't really consider it rape. I think he leave her very confuse. About men I mean.


*2/10/86*

The dean's secretary mentioned the other day that grievance procedure is outlined in the *University Handbook* (which functions as CSU's constitution). I dropped by the library reference room to take a look.

Most of the information was shrouded in legalistic jargon but I did learn a little. The grievance hearing seems to proceed much like a court trial, except that, in place of judge and jury there are three judges (the Grievance Committee). Grievance decisions are binding within the university, but do not affect my right to sue later.

I noticed the heading "Grading Policy" in the table of contents, so I skimmed that section. Found something extremely interesting—article 113.22e—which reads: "classroom instructors are responsible for determining and recording all course grades."

Plain and unequivocal, isn't it? Classroom instructors, not departments, determine grades. It's right in our bleeding constitution. Any teacher has authority to do exactly what I did. Instructors are in fact *required* to determine their students' grades. Article 113.22e will help at my hearing I do believe. It can help other instructors too—once they know about it.

The stories are almost done. Just one to go. The reworking has been fairly easy, and the collection now has much greater coherence. Can't think why I opposed a single narrator.

*Tuesday, February 11*
Today Dr. Braeme return our papers on "New Narcissists." Again I receive C–.

He write only few comment this time. He say my writing contain many grammars, especially verbs. He mention nothing about my arguments, but I think he dont like them much if he give C– grade. Lower than that and I must repeat 101 because D grade is not passing.

For our next paper he want us to explain what Hemingway mean in his story "A Clean, Well-Lighted Place." To me it is clear assignment. I think I can do it. Also, from what Dr. Braeme say in class, he seem to understand story same way as me. Maybe for once he will like what I write.

This is out of class paper so I can take time with it, revise it, correct my grammars. Perhaps I can get B. That is my goal. I don't expect higher than B on any English paper. But with B, I can pull up my C– grades.

There is one paragraph in Hemingway's story that still confuse me. Tomorrow, if Mr. Goddard come in lab, I will ask him.

Tet ends today. I offer fruit and rice at my shrine, light incense, and make a prayer. But I don't feel better. For some reason my family is far away.

*2/12/86*
Braeme is asking Tina and her classmates to interpret "A Clean, Well-Lighted Place." She was having trouble understanding the passage where Hemingway uses all the nadas.

I focused her on those. She knew the meaning of "nada," but hadn't quite clicked on its significance for the story. I asked if she recognized the prayer Hemingway was fooling with.

"The Pater Noster."

"Right. So why does the older waiter put all the nadas in the Pater Noster?"

She thought about it. "He say God is nothing. He is atheist, I think."

"And why is he atheist?"

That stopped her. She read back over the paragraph, frowning. She took it to her desk, sat down, cogitated.

In ten minutes she was back. "It's because he's lonely and frightened, and he lose everything of value in his life. He lose faith even in God."

She may not quite have her thesis yet but she certainly has a grasp of the story. I think she can nail this one. It just worries me that she seems a little lethargic.

Probably she's discouraged. She got her second paper back from Braeme, with another C–, a grade that seems to me too low given the quality of her arguments. Sure, she made some verb mistakes, but not enough to take the grade below a B. My opinion. Oddly, old Danny didn't say word one about her ideas. He really isn't clear about why he graded so low.

We'll see if her Hemingway paper polishes his apple. If she does A work (as I think she will) and gets yet another C–, we'll know he has it in for her. There's still time to drop.


*Thursday, February 13*

For last two nights I dream about that man who keep me in cave. I dream it just how it happen. I hear his cigarette cough in the dark, his feet crunch the dirt. I am tie with rope, but I can roll on floor of cave to get away. He feel for me with his arms, speaking his language. I can see much better than him, because he enter cave from the sun.

Then he light match and now he can see me. Smiling, he walk over, look down at me as match burn out and cave is dark again. I know he will not light another match. I feel sick. Soon he will untie my legs and do it to me again until he is tired, which takes a long time. He is not clean, I hate his sweat and cigarette stink, it hurts what he does.

Worst thing, as long as I live he will never leave my mind. He is part of me, like my skin.

*2/14/86*

Last class I gave back Roberto's second paper—an NC+. Same failing grade as before, and same reason: unclear sentences. After class he came up and wanted to discuss the sentences I'd marked. Could I explain why they were unclear?

Ignoring the edge in his voice, I picked one of the worst offenders. It was a rat maze of a main clause that rambled on for half a page, paused for breath at a semicolon, then staggered to the end of the page and beyond, burdened by a prolix, effusive, and rambunctious vocabulary. I asked him to read the sentence aloud.

He began with confidence and grave purpose, but as anyone would have soon became snarled in his sticky web of words. He stumbled, stumbled again, had to start over. This time he made it through, but not without several revealing missteps. In the end, he had to agree with me that the sentence had problems. "So how should I write it?" he asked.

"More like you talk. Shorter sentences. Simpler vocabulary." I showed him how to break his one long sentence into four, then crossed out redundancies and substituted common words for his throbbing purple orchids of the lexicon.

"So plain," he said as I was finishing. "Sounds like third grade."

"Well, if you want, we can pump it up a little." I combined two of my third grade sentences into one and notched up the diction a little, trying to retain clarity.

He read that version several times, without a word. He pointed to another sentence I'd marked. "Do that one."

I did it.

He studied. "Not bad," he admitted.

"You try one." I pointed to a half-page briar patch. I left him with it as I cleaned the blackboard, packed my things, reviewed lesson plans for my next class. When I checked on what he had, it was pretty damn good, a little wordy maybe, but much clearer.

"You're getting it," I told him. "Try another."

This time I watched as he rewrote one sentence as three. The last of those, I must say, was eloquent.

Sometimes, with the clarity thing, you see this kind of near-instant cure. But we'll have to watch for relapse. The root of the problem can be buried deep in the writer's personality and, if so, relapse is to be expected.


*Sunday, February 16*
On Friday morning Rayneece go to school with her books. More than two days I don't see her, then this afternoon she come home in same clothes, carry her books, look very tired with red sleepy eyes.

I'm glad she's okay, because I worry. Sometimes she go out with a guy and disappear, but never before does she go to school and disappear. Here is her explanation. Between classes on Friday she run into Neal her old boyfriend in Student Union. He ask her to go to Las Vegas. So she did it!

Now she's sleeping. She was awake for more than 50 hours so she will sleep for a long time. I hope Neal is not her boyfriend again. Didn't she already figure out he's not so wonderful?


*2/17/86*
Saw a lawyer this evening—Michael Smitherman. He's just up the street. Although he was fully scheduled, he told me to come in after closing, at 6:30. Good sign right there.

We met for half an hour—at no charge. His office is on the second floor of a restored Victorian house, across the hall from a dentist. When I walked in I recognized him right away. I've seen him out on the porch, in the same or a similar tan corduroy suit, talking to neighborhood folks, his clients I guess. He's tall, a little overweight, with sandy thinning hair and liquid brown eyes. We shook hands and he took me into his office. Everyone else had gone home.

I showed him the letter from the Promotion and Retention Committee and explained what the change in my ranking means— that I'm out of a job. He says I was right to file the grievance.

Next we discussed what the English Department can use against me to prove I'm an insubordinate instructor who overidentifies with his students and abuses colleagues. I told him about the grade changes I did for Tina and Araceli, explained why I thought they were the real reason for my lowered ranking. I also showed him the page I xeroxed from the *University Handbook* with Article 113.22e highlighted. He thinks it should help us.

Maybe most important, he accepted my portrayal of CSUM's writing program as a massive flunkout mechanism, directed (intentionally or unintentionally) at lower economic classes and new immigrants. He wasn't even surprised, I think because he represents clients who could be from the families of my students. Like me, he's seen up close the barriers society tends to erect against such people. I really need a lawyer with that knowledge—and some commitment.

The bad news is I have to pay him out of my own pocket. He can't do it on contingency because I'm not asking for any money in the grievance—only restoration of former rank. His usual rate is $125/hour, but he's agreed to do it for half since he believes in the cause (he said). He's going to start by deposing Tina, Araceli and me sometime next week.

I'm assuming that Araceli and Tina want to get involved. Have to call them and see. They've got to back it 100% or we won't proceed.


*Tuesday, February 18*
Mr. Goddard call to tell me the English Department is try to fire him and he must fight to keep his job. There will be a hearing, he ask can I speak for him there, maybe read the best paper I write for his class.

"Are they firing you because you change my grade?"

"Partly that. But for other reasons too."

I tell him I want to help any way I can. Araceli is going to help too. We will all meet with lawyer next Monday to talk.

Then he ask about the check he give me, did I cash it yet?

I could tell a lie, but I know he will catch me later. So I tell the truth, that I burn it for good luck. I also explain why I cannot take money for help my friend. I expect he will argue me, but no, he listen to my reasons without one word. He accept my position.

I feel he is unusual American. He makes effort to consider other ideas than the ones already in his mind. In result, he has better manners than many of his countrymen.


*2/19/86*

Eurylochus is right when he calls Odysseus a daredevil willing to sacrifice the lives of his men in pursuit of personal glory. Odysseus reveals this heroic warp several times in his showdown with Polyphemus.

Picture this. The Greek sailors have just found paradise: an idyllic island offering docile and succulent goats, delicious fruits of the vine, spring water, everything they need. As they sit down to their first feast in Eden, they hear the Cyclopes tribe going about business on an adjacent island. Odysseus, curious, decides to find out what kind of folks these are, whether they are law abiding and hospitable, or brutal savages.

He takes some men and sails across the channel to spy on Polyphemus, at work in his yard. The Cyclops is so huge and rough hewn he reminds Odysseus of a wooded mountain standing solitary in the sky. The Greek leader fears the creature is ferocious and utterly without rules, yet nonetheless decides to go hang out in Polyphemus' cave with his men. He hopes big buddy, on his return, will graciously favor them with food, drink, and gifts.

Possessing an imperfect grasp of Greek hospitality, Polyphemus, when he discovers the intruders in his home, dines them not, but instead dines upon them, two to a meal. He bashes their brains out on his cave floor, tears them limb from limb, devouring them raw, bones and entrails too, with the table manners of a crocodile.

Chips down, Odysseus of course leaps into action. He blinds the monster and escapes with most of his scouting party. They set sail in their boat and soon are safe—until their vainglorious king decides to bellow his victory over the waves to his enraged opponent on shore. Blind Polyphemus uses Odysseus' voice to aim broken-off mountain peaks, twice almost sinking the Greek ship.

Still not satisfied, wanting full credit for his deeds, Odysseus yells to the monster his exact identity—name, lineage, and home island. Polyphemus later uses this information in a prayer to his father Poseidon, requesting punishment for those who took his only eye. Poseidon wipes out Odysseus' entire fleet, killing his remaining men. Only Odysseus survives.

It is an instructive story, one Odysseus, Jr. should keep in mind. No good leader will place his troops in peril for personal reasons only. Putting your own ass in a sling is one thing; making your friends pay for you is another.

Tried running today up on the track. Took it slow. Wheezed through ten laps, then walked home.

The old bod feels good tonight—tired and lazy, ready for bed. Seems I'm bouncing back.


*Thursday, February 20*

Today Dr. Braeme return our papers on "A Clean, Well Lighted Place." All except mine. He ask me to stay after class so we can talk.

As the other students leave, I go to him. He is putting away his books and pretend he does not see me. I speak his name.

"Ah, Miss Le," he say. "I have questions about your paper. Do you mind?"

Even though I will be late to next class, I must find out what it is about. The way he look at me I think I must be in trouble.

He pick up my paper, turn pages, read a sentence which contain the word isolation. He ask, "Could you define isolation?"

"To be alone."

"Is that all?"

"That's what it mean to me."

"I see," he say, looking disappoint. He find another word I write—alienated—ask me to define it.

I tell him my meaning, but that is wrong too, I guess, because he look even more disappoint. Then he ask me questions about the Pater Noster, about nada, and about a lot of other stuff. I give him my answers, but he doesn't like any of them. He look mad. The bottom of his ears are red.

"Miss Le," he say, "you seem to have rather poor grasp of your own ideas. Why I wander?"

"I don't know." How can I answer such question?

"You don't know? You write this closely reason, well express essay with few grammars, a paper totally unlike your first two, but you don't know how you did it?"

"I know how."

"It's someone else's work isn't it?"

"No, it's mine."

"Nobody help you write it?"

"No."

"I find this hard to believe."

Well, he has decide the truth for himself already. Let him believe what he want. I don't even answer.

He say if that's my final position, that nobody help me write it, he will have to consider carefully what grade to give. He put my paper in his briefcase. He will return it later, he say.

I wonder, can he fail my paper just because he is suspicious?

I almost call Mr. Goddard to learn his thoughts on these troubling matters. Then I realize, no, that would not be smart. What if he get angry with Professor Braeme and start a big fight? Who would that help? And isn't Mr. Goddard in enough trouble already?

So I didn't call.


*2/21/86*

Danny boy came in my office this afternoon as I was grading papers. He had Tina Le's Hemingway essay in hand. Wanted me, as her former teacher, to read it.

Well, I did, and it's a terrific paper. The best expository prose I've seen from her. Lucidly argued, gracefully written. Powerful in its understated emotions—much like the narrative essay she did for my class. In short, Wow.

There I was, feeling terrific because I thought old Dan was sharing a pedogogical triumph with me, teacher to teacher. A look-at-what-our-student-has-accomplished sort of thing. I figured he saw, as I did, that she'd just made a big breakthrough. His question caught me off guard.

"Do you think she wrote it?" His small hazel eyes were framed in the top panels of his bifocals. In his eyes I noticed two things I had not noticed before: little black flecks and terminal stupidity.

"Of course she wrote it."

"Without assistance?"

"She may have gone to the Writing Center for help with the verbs. And she discussed the assignment with me briefly. But beyond that—"

"—She discussed it with you?"

"We talked about one thing. Why Hemingway put Spanish words in the Lord's Prayer."

"She swore up and down she had no help with the paper, from anyone. Now you say you helped her. And maybe others in the Writing Center helped her. What am I to believe?"

"She wrote the paper. Believe it."

"You didn't help her with the wording?"

"Not in the least."

"You know, John, you have a reputation for backing your students all the way."

"Could you tell me why you think she didn't write it?"

"It's the ideas, sir, the ideas. A girl who has proven mediocre in her conceptual thinking on previous assignments suddenly blossoms into a mature intellect. What am I to assume? I'm not accustomed to such instant transformations. Perhaps they are run of the mill for charismatic teachers such as yourself, but not in my experience."

"Which ideas in the paper aren't hers?"

"Which ones are hers would be the question. And the second question would be, in whose style is the paper couched? Certainly not hers."

For half an hour I tried to persuade him. I asked how dumb Tina could be—with an A average in math. I dragged out my copy of her story "Minh and Dao," read him parts of it, offered to copy it all for him so he could read it at leisure. But I guess he thought I wrote the story for her too, because he dismissed it as irrelevant.

"You seem to know a great deal about this girl," he said with a hard stare.

The shithead. In his prejudiced arrogance he really believes Tina couldn't have written the paper. Just because it's good.


*Saturday, February 22*
Mr. Goddard phone this morning, say Dr. Braeme talk to him about my paper. Braeme thinks Mr. Goddard write the paper for me.

I am so stupid to try hard on that assignment: plan with pages of notes, write four drafts, check the grammars many times, try not to make one error when I type. All this work, and in result I convince Professor Braeme I must be cheating.

I want to drop his class. But now I can't. The rule is if you drop while failing, you fail. So I must wait for Dr. Braeme's decision on my paper. If he pass the paper, then I can drop.

If I must stay in his class, I know how to write my papers now. I will agree with everything my teacher think, as far as I can guess, and on each paper I will try to write C– level, which he believe I can. That way, if I pass final, I will reach my goal—successful completion of English 101.

Here's something interesting. Dr. Braeme knows Mr. Goddard was my 002 teacher, but who tell him? We didn't.

*2/23/86*

Had a whole new kind of nightmare last night. A knuckle ball. I'm in a huge college lecture hall with several hundred students. On my desk a sealed exam booklet. The cover reads—

EXPIRY 455

FINAL EXAM

Terror grips my galloping heart. I can't recall even one meeting of this class, or any text. I do vaguely remember signing up, but beyond that nothing. Yet here I am seated for the final. Ignorant of all course subject matter. Panicking.

Someones shouts "Begin!" and I break the seal on the booklet. Inside the cover I find this caution: ANSWER EACH QUESTION ACCURATELY AND COMPLETELY ON PENALTY OF DEATH. Many pages of questions follow, and under each question are several long blanks, inviting detailed answers.

Here are the three questions on page 1:

1) What living beings have you killed with your mouth?

2) What living beings have you killed with your eyes?

3) What living beings have you killed with your facial hair?

I flip through the booklet. Every body part seems to be covered in the same way.

Because the clock is ticking, I go back to the first question and try to figure out how to answer it. But can I ever know, for instance, the number of tiny insects I've killed over a lifetime with my mouth—while eating fruits and other uncooked foods...while riding my bike as a kid...while running? And how identify my victims, as the question seems to require? Most are long forgotten.

The more I think about it, the more any answer seems impossible. I sit with pencil frozen, mind racing in circles.

Then I wake up.

Another spooky one. Except for the killing theme, it's a dream you might expect of a college student.

*Monday, February 24*

Mr. Goddard take Araceli and me to see the lawyer as we agree, but the lawyer is not there. We wait one hour. Then lawyer walk in on his bare socks, carry his shoes. He explain he must drive all the way from Sherman Oaks and that's why he's late. But I still do not understand why he carry his shoes. Maybe he prefer to drive in his socks.

He take Mr. Goddard in his office and they talk. Soon Mr. Goddard come out again. He say let's go. And we leave.

On the way home, he explain to us the lawyer is too busy now to take his case. I can see our teacher is angry, but he tries not to show. He apologize for wasting our time.

Araceli say no problem. She say he must find better lawyer, she will be glad to do it again.

I say same. For sure my teacher must get better lawyer than this one.

Then I remember what I want to ask Araceli: did she take English 101, and who is her teacher? I am curious because maybe they trick her like me, put her in class with unfair teacher.

She didn't sign up for 101. She will wait till her 002 grade is certain. Wish I was smart like that.


2/24/86

Smitherman's a frigging fruit loop. Dropped me like a hot potato—without the courtesy of a phone call.

I'm still trying to understand it. Normally a lawyer will accept someone's money. It's almost instinctive, isn't it? They are among the most accepting of all professionals, I have heard. So why aren't my bucks good enough for this bozo?

In checking out my grievance did he poke his nose into something threatening, something he thinks may be out of his league? Why do I get the feeling he chickened? The look on his face, I guess.

One thing is certain. Shoeless Mike Smitherman is not the man for the job. Right politics perhaps, but as I couldn't help noticing today he has the kind of liquid eyes that are drowning. Liquid eyes can be fine, but they must swim, not sink.

Christ almighty. Now I've got to track down another legal beagle.


*Tuesday, February 25*

Today after class Braeme talk to me again about my Hemingway paper. He tell me he find out from Mr. Goddard that I have help with it, against what I tell him before. It is plagiarism, he say, which means the work is not mine, therefore it must fail. If I do it again, he will fail me for the course.

Then he give the paper back to me. I see F on top and these words: "On future assignments, please rely on your own ideas and expression."

Even though I expect him to criticize me, it makes me so angry when he tell me paper is not mine. It's so unfair! But what can I say? I excuse myself, go to my next class.

Naturally I'm late, and because I am furious I find I can't concentrate on the quiz Dr. Parviz give us. I solve the problems, but not with full attention, and I didn't have time to check even one answer. If I do well, lucky me.

At home, Rayneece notice my bad mood, ask what's the matter? I tell her about what's happening to me—and to Mr. Goddard too. We talk about it for some time.

Rayneece say, since it's the English Department, she's not really surprise. In her opinion, theres not much I can do if they want to fail me, because I'm just a student. But she say Mr. Goddard must fight back because he can win. With a good lawyer, she say.

I tell her about the lawyer we visit on Saturday.

That's not a lawyer, she say, that's ambulance chaser.

Then she remember this guy she know. He's a lawyer. She thinks he might be interested in Mr. Goddard's case. He is bright person, very mature and hard worker, she say. He used to go to CSUM.

Is he some old boyfriend of Rayneece's I wander? Will he be dependable? I ask how she knows him.

"He use to date my sister."

Is that better? I don't even know her sister.

Finally I decide to let my teacher choose. He can talk to the guy and find out if he's any good.

2/26/86

The editors of *Paved River Review* sent Tina's story back to me with this note scribbled on the title page: "Regrets. Space limitations make it impossible for us to include this piece."

Space limitations, my ass. Danny boy is behind this. Got to be him because of the timing, and because I told him the story had been accepted. He must have convinced the magazine staff I wrote it. Maybe he believes that.

Not sure how Tina will feel about this. Publication doesn't seem to mean much to her, so I don't guess she'll be too disappointed.

Some good news, maybe. Tina's roommate, whom I haven't met, seems to have found someone to represent me. Arvin Ledford. Graduated UCLA Law School last spring and passed the bar in the summer. Doesn't have any trial experience, but because of that he's hungry. He's been doing freelance legal research.

Commitment to the cause is Arvin's strong suit. Four years ago he failed English 101 for the second time and flunked out of CSUM. So he's a victim of the system. He wants to use my hearing to publicize what's going on in our writing program—and he's quite open about that. But I see no problem since his agenda fits well with mine.

I like Arvin. He seems real to me. And, unlike Shoeless Mike, he appears to be a fighter. The first time he failed 101 he took it to the Humper and they went twelve rounds. He raised so much hell the case ended up being adjudicated by the University Senate. Perhaps not surprisingly, that clan of aging professors decided against him.

"And the second time you failed?"

He continued in his soft precise voice, with a slight lisp. "That was different. Hit me a lot harder. I was out of school all of a sudden, in debt for student loans, my basketball scholarship gone. My confidence was gone too.

"Not my self-confidence, thank god, but my confidence in the system. I could see, or thought I could see—19 years old remember—that the man wasn't going to let me succeed, however hard I worked for it. The man wanted me in one of three places. In a servile job. In jail. Or in my grave."

"You didn't fight it?"

"I did something really stupid. I followed that professor bitch to her car one afternoon, found out where she parked. The next week, same day, same time, I was waiting for her in my car parked not far away. I had one of my mom's nylon stockings to pull over my head and my little brother's string knife that he used on his paper route—wicked looking blade. Think I was planning to scare her, but I don't really know."

"She didn't come back to her car?"

"While I was waiting, one of the cheerleaders saw me and came over to commiserate. She'd heard I flunked out. Talking to her helped me get a grip on reality. After she left, so did I."

Arvin's lack of experience could be a problem, but it's the only negative I see. His dedication is strong and since he doesn't have other cases he can focus all his energy on mine. For advice, when he really needs it, he can draw on his law school friends, maybe his old professors. His rates are good too—70 bucks an hour.

*Thursday, February 27*

Today Mr. Goddard phone to tell me my story will not be publish in our school magazine. For some reason they don't want it now. He say these things happen. He wants to send it to other magazines. This seems important to him, so I say yes.

Roberto get back his third paper from Mr. Goddard with grade he want: CR+. He is so excited, show it to me, make me read Mr. Goddard's strong comments. I'm happy for him. But it is what I expect when smart guy like Roberto get a good teacher. Too bad I can't have such luck in my English class.

*3/1/86*

I thought Arvin and I wouldn't have enough privacy on campus so we met at my place. We worked all afternoon, got a lot done.

He seems to think we have a fairly strong case, though we won't know for sure till he compares my job credentials with other faculty. His disclosure rights give him access to all the job files in the English Dept. He needs to find out more about CSU's grievance procedure too. Somebody he knows at UCLA handled a grievance on another Cal State campus a few years back, and Arvin wants to talk to him.

When we got hungry we adjourned to Mario's. Together we wasted a large pizza and three or four pitchers of beer. Got to talking about our army experiences. His were long after Vietnam of course.

Turns out he developed his interest in law while serving. After basic, his high test scores got him assigned to the legal staff at Fort Benning where he worked as a paralegal helping attorneys prep cases for trial. In that sense he does have trial experience. He's just never argued in court.

It was dark when we walked back. My attorney seemed to be weaving a little on the sidewalk, though some of that may have been in the eye of the beholder.

At his car he climbed in, rolled down the window, fired the engine and saluted. "Later, Sergeant Goddard."

"Motate with caution, Sergeant Ledford. Better hit your lights."

He rectified the oversight, saluted again, then drove away straight, very straight, confirming my faith in his sobriety.

My kind of lawyer—the man can hold his mead.


*Saturday, March 1*

This morning Rayneece get her hairs style at a shop in Baldwin Park. She come back with new dress, spend the whole afternoon polish her fingernails, toenails, do her face. She take one hour for her face only! When I see this—I know there is a new man.

After she is dressed and ready, she must wait long time for him to arrive. She sit on couch in front of television, chew her pink fingernail and frown. He must be quite late, I decide, because I never see her wait like this before. Finally, almost 10:00 PM, somebody knock on door. Rayneece ask me to answer it while she "get ready." She go in her room.

The guy is tall, with a beard and glasses. He introduce himself as Arvid something. He seems nice, but his eyes are quite red and he smell strongly of alcohol.

I ask him please sit on couch, then I tell Rayneece through her door he's arrive. I go in my room to stay out of it.

Rayneece make him wait 20 minutes before she come out. He apologize to her for be so late, and he sound sincere. She accept his apology but she is not happy with him. I can hear in her voice.

After they leave, I think about his excuse. He say he is with Mr. Goddard, working on the hearing, and there is no phone in restaurant. I must wander, is this the lawyer that will help my teacher? And does he drink like this frequently? What does Mr. Goddard think of his drinking, because he was there and see it for himself.

This worry me.


3/4/86

Tina saw me running in the stadium this afternoon and stopped to say hello. From her cultural perspective, I realized, running in public with shorts on—at my age—probably ranks borderline insane. Of course she knows Americans are loony. Out of curiosity I think, she asked why I did it.

I gave my reasons, but she looked skeptical. I began to feel embarrassed. Here I was trying to justify something that seems a little absurd to me too. Finally I told her it's hard to understand what running's like without doing it. To my amazement, she interpreted that as an invitation to join me some time.

Well, why not? She might like it, and it's fun having company. She looks like she's in good shape. Must walk a lot. I don't envision her collapsing after a lap or two, anything like that.

She told me she just dropped Braeme's class. She figured he was going to fail her no matter what. I can see her point. What I regret is she's giving up one of her chances to pass 101.

Can't say I didn't contribute to her mess: so in love with old Danny was I, so smitten with the avuncular image he projects in his well-tailored tweed.

*Tuesday, March 4*

Yesterday as I walk home I see man on track running. He look familiar. Is it possible? I go to fence and wait till he come to my end. Yes, it's Mr. Goddard. He wear soaking wet Hard Rock Cafe T-shirt and shorts! I wave so he see me.

He stop running, walk off track to where I am. He hook fingers through fence, breath hard and drip his sweat everywhere. His face is red, he looks extremely hot. His hairs are sweated to his scalp.

I notice his hair is not all brown, as I think, some is red. Much easier to see the red hairs in the sun. A little drop of water hang on his nose, shake as he breath. He have very strong leg muscles—like my brother. Something you can never see with pants on. His arms are strong too.

I ask why he run so hard. It seem like he punish himself.

First reason, he say, is keep body healthy. Second, running is good way to relief the pressures of the day. Last, it help you sleep better at night.

Those are all good reasons, and the last one—better sleep— make me think running could be worth it for sure. So when he invite me to do it, I say yes. Try one time, I decide, see if you like.

Dr. Parviz return our quizzes today. I receive C+. That is my lowest grade *ever* in math or science. Fortunately, it is quiz only, not midterm, so it won't hurt my course grade that much. And since I drop English I have more time to study.

*3/5/86*

Got a call from Kratzer today. He likes the manuscript and is asking for only minor changes. Maybe a couple day's work. Good news indeed.

Publication will be next January. I'll have to do a book tour early in the year.

I'm glad to have this one in the bank. It should help me at the hearing. I don't believe anyone else in the Department has published a book for some years. Cecil edited the collection of essays, but that's a little different.

*Thursday, March 6*

I run with my teacher today and find it fun mostly—except I make mistake. I wear tennis shoes because I think the rubber bottoms will be good traction.

Mr. Goddard warn me tennis shoes can hurt my feet. I say don't worry, because I think it can't matter much. Later, when my foot feel pain, I think no problem. It does not hurt bad, and the other foot does not hurt at all.

Later my foot hurt greatly and my teacher notice me limping. He make me sit on grass, take off shoe. The toe of my sock is red. Inside, we find blisters on all my toes. The blister on my big toe is broke and bleeding.

Mr. Goddard walk home with me. I go slow with my shoe off, it take us a long time. After we reach Rayneece and my apartment, he come upstairs. He ask about medicine stuffs, but I'm looking at dirty dishes in sink, messy apartment which hasn't been clean for week. Then I remember, Rayneece keep tube of medicine to kill germs in bathroom. But it is necessary for blisters? My teacher say yes, he know somebody get bad infection from blisters.

While I sit in chair, he run hot water in sink, soak end of little towel and he clean my foot. I am embarrass. In my country a man does not touch woman on foot unless they are marry. I try to tell myself he is just like doctor, but still I feel uncomfortable as he put on the medicine, tape bandage to my toe.

"You look a little flushed," he say. "Do you have a fever?"

"Running make me warm," I say.

He look at me kind of funny.

Then I realize, how can I be warm from running, so long after? But how can I tell him the real reason? Finally he finish and I relax.

To be polite, I offer tea.

Iced water is what he wants. Water makes sense after running, I guess, but I don't like the ice. I leave it out of mine.

He ask about Vietnam, do I miss it? I talk about that awhile. Mainly, I tell him about Grandfather, partly because Mr. Goddard remind me of him. They are alike in one important way—they both will do the right thing, even if everybody is against them. And when they fight for their belief, fire shine in their eyes. Guys like that are brave men, but a little frightening.

I ask about his family, but all he will tell me is he hasn't seen them in 15 years. He's not even sure they are alive.

It's hard for me to understand. He doesn't seem to hate them. Is he hiding from them? But why would he do that?


3/7/86

Tina has ability as a runner. I set a slow pace thinking she'd need it, but after a while I had to step it up because I could see she was chopping her stride. She did two miles without strain. Would have done more, but she developed some bad blisters.

The blisters were my fault. I let her run in her topsiders, when I knew better. Must say though she has grit. Turned her big toe to hamburger without a peep.

After I dressed her foot (at her place) we talked a while. She told me how her grandfather died. Quite a story. He founded and for many years managed a successful wholesale electrical supply in Can Tho. Because of his wealth and political connections with the old regime, he was not popular with the communists when they came to power. He was treated very harshly, despite his 70+ years.

His business and virtually all his personal property was seized by the state. He was arrested, tried, and convicted of selling war supplies to the Americans. Since he had, in the state's eyes, "enriched himself on the blood and bones of the Vietnamese people," he was sent to a re-education camp to learn the teachings of Uncle Ho.

The family feared for his life because health conditions in the camps were notorious. Physical and psychological torture were the main methods of instruction. For six months, no word from or about Grandpa. Then a letter arrived in his handwriting. It was filled with glowing reports of camp life. He was ecstatic to be absorbing the great truths of Uncle Ho.

The family knew Grandpa Le hated Ho Chi Minh, to the extent he couldn't walk past the huge obligatory living room portrait of Uncle without a rude gesture. So between the lines lay his message: life in the camp was dreadful, censorship absolute.

The family heard nothing more for a year. Word finally came during a visit from a former business associate of Grandfather's who'd been "re-educated" in the same camp. During a cholera outbreak, Grandpa organized a medical team and petitioned the camp administration for sanitary drinking water and rudimentary medical supplies. He used the argument "Dead men can't sip from Uncle Ho's fountain of wisdom."

The camp administration rewarded his activism with a public execution, attended by the whole camp. The executioners were select inmate "volunteers." That was all the friend would say. He left the mode of execution unspoken—and the family didn't really want to know.

In the way Tina talks about him, it's obvious she and her grandfather were very close.


*Sunday, March 9*
I study all weekend for midterms in Matrix Theory and Calculus. Not much time to write in here.

My goal is: A on both tests, prove I can do something right.

*3/10/86*

During office hours, a 200-pound crewcut with an earring and an attitude appeared in my doorway. "John Goddard?"

"Correct."

"Zane Gorak, Maravilla Student Times. You filed a grievance?"

"Most surely."

"The English Department's reasons for dusting you are pretty general. What were you up to? Dorking the jailbait?"

"Nothing so rewarding."

"What then?"

I began explaining the two grade changes I'd done as he came out of his slouch, entered the office, sat down on Ralph's desk. Reslouching, he opened a small notebook and commenced to write. "Basically, in the case of two students, you told the English Department to shove its final exam."

"Basically that's it."

"Then what happened?"

I went through the repercussions in detail, from the warning letters to my lowered ranking.

He smiled, shook his head. "Know what I think? I think you deserve a medal, dude. Those squirrelly finals have wiped out more of my friends than I care to count. Take my girlfriend. A double E major. 3.5 GPA. Speaks four languages. Won essay contests as a kid in Hong Kong. Then she gets some dipshit in elbow patches for English 002 and fails. Now she's scared to take it again for fear of flunking out of school."

He stood up and ambled, gesturing with his arms. "She's twice as bright as me, man. Works three times as hard. But she's quite probably going to flunk out of THIS FUCKING RATHOLE INSTITUTION ON ACCOUNT OF A FUCKING ENGLISH COURSE!"

I had to calm him down before he could continue the interview. I closed the door to keep his voice from echoing down the hall.

"I'll tell you one thing," he said, seated on the desk again. "She's a hell of a lot brighter than that dickhead professor she had. I used to wait outside the class, heard him lecture. The man was ignorant.

He talked in a monotone, read right out of the textbook. Like they couldn't read or something."

He heaved an almighty sigh and I got a whiff of brewery breath. Then he was off again: "I'd like to see that twit learn Chinese perfectly in four years, like he expected her to do with English. After four years, I'll bet he couldn't talk his way into a blow job at a Shanghai cat house. Let me tell you what he—"

I motioned to hold it down.

"Sorry," he said, massaging his temples. "I'm a little passionate on the subject."

I approached indirectly. "You don't want this story to sound biased, right? You want to sound objective."

"Right on, Batman. This story will be so pissing objective the Pope will bless it."

"It's crucial."

"I hear you."

"Do you know how much space we'll get?"

His eyes went hard. "My editor has the say on that. No promises."


*Wednesday, March 12*

I think I do good on my midterms. But tonight I almost don't care. It's enough to have them finish. No homeworks at all, how wonderful! I can be lazy, watch TV, fix big Vietnamese dinner for Rayneece and me.

It is my night to fix dinner. Now we trade every Wednesday. I have to think careful because sometime she does not like certain dishes. One thing she always go for—dumpling. Any kind, she love it.

Today in Student Union I walk by the room with the table tennis players. As usual, every table is fill. Sometimes I feel I want to go in there, play maybe, but I don't ever have time. Besides, I see few women in there. Guys mostly, very serious about the game.

In Vietnam I love to play table tennis. We play in school, and I play with my brother till I can beat him. Winning him is quite difficult because of his bigger size and athletic nature. But my hand is just a little faster than his hand, and I know how to make him lose his temper. By the time I'm 14, these are the weapons I use to defeat him frequently. Oh how he hate me when I win!

At 15, I join team and sometimes there are matches and we go to tournaments across the city. One afternoon I go to tournament with friends. No problem until we come home. The three of us are talking, not pay attention, get on wrong bus. Nobody notice till we travel many kilometers in the wrong direction, outside town. We have to get off at country store, wait for another bus which take hours to come. When we get home, it is quite late.

Usually my parents never show their temper, but that night they blow up. Both of them yell at me. They say I must be exactly on time every day, not one minute late, or else I might not have a family. Father explain he buy places for us on boat that will take us out of Vietnam. Any night can be the one we leave, and we must be ready in minutes.

Mother say, "Your old enough to understand. We must rely on you now."

Well, from that night my happy child life is over. I just didn't know it yet.

*3/12/86*

Zane's story on my grievance got a two-column spread on page 1 and took up half of page 6. The headline was written large: ENGLISH INSTRUCTOR LOSES JOB FOR OVERTURNING 002 FAILURES. No way to miss it.

When Zane interviewed Minter and the Hump he managed to provoke them into some very defensive comments about why they pressured me to fail Tina and Araceli, and about the failure rates in the writing program generally. As he promised, it all sounds objective, yet any intelligent reader will understand that an instructor is being railroaded by vindictive administrators for defending two of his students.

Those who hate and/or fear the English Department (about

90% of our student body) should find the information intriguing. I can't imagine better publicity for us. The students of course won't decide my grievance—three tenured professors will. But I think student awareness is important. The Grievance Committee will find it much harder to screw me.

Walking home across campus late in the day I looked in three newspaper distribution boxes hoping to pick up another copy of the paper. Every box was empty. Never seen that before. Could be a good sign.


*Thursday, March 13*

In the mail we get advertisement from sports store. They sell running shoes 1/2 off. Since I don't know about such shoes, I phone Mr. Goddard for advice.

He kindly offer to take me to store. He think it is best for us both to look at the shoes, so he can advice me directly. Fortunately it is not far.

We examine many shoes. Finally I buy some that are made for woman's foot and for running. According to salesman, they will protect my feet from blisters and other injuries. Usually these shoes cost $59.95, but on sale they are $33 with tax.

They are blue, quite attractive. They feel soft and light on my feet. I am quite please with them. Besides running in these shoes, I can wear them with my jeans to school. So no money has been waste, even if I don't run very much.


*3/14/86*

Received official notice of my grievance hearing in the mail. Starts March 25th, the first Tuesday after spring break. That's less than two weeks from now, much sooner than we expected. Maybe they figure we won't be ready.

The place is Administration 844. Eighth floor of ADM is the penthouse, with the President's suite and I don't really know what else. Never been up there.

I have heard rumors. The one about the world-class wet bar I mostly believe. The one about the foldout bed I do but partly believe.

There must be conference rooms, vice presidents' offices maybe.

Soon we'll see.

*Sunday, March 16*

Arvin and Rayneece have first argument last night. First one I hear anyway. She want to go to Santa Barbara for little vacation. He don't.

"You been working like a dog," she say. "You need some rest. You got all spring break to get ready for the hearing."

"It's your spring break," he answer. "I don't get any spring break."

"If you can't give me two days of your precious time, see you in a week. Cause I'm going."

I expect him to yell at her. Instead he just push air out of his mouth, don't say a word.

Today they leave for Santa Barbara.

*3/16/86*

When I was in the library today, I dropped by the Bierce books and poked around again. Came across an old volume I overlooked earlier—one with a marble cover and rough-cut pages. Published in 1922. Never been checked out. It's a collection of Bierce's letters written during the last years of his life.

Read about half this afternoon. So far I'm a little disappointed. The majority of the correspondence is to poet George Sterling, one of Bierce's protegés. Bierce's letters are devoted primarily to critiques of Sterling's pretentious, conventional and wordy poems, which Bierce undertook to edit by mail.

I've started skimming. Want to get to the end, where letters to Sterling taper off and letters to others predominate.

Very hot today so I saved exercise for evening. Took a long walk around the neighborhood. I've always liked evening best. As traffic falls off and streetlights begin to glow, birds streak close overhead, too dark to identify except by silhouette. A slender moon is rising above a darkened office building. From open, lighted windows the sounds of silverware on plates, people talking, a blathering TV. The air cooling as it fills with night.

Passed Tina's house. A light was on in her window. Studying, I bet.

*Monday, March 17*

After work I run with Mr. Goddard. My new shoes are excellent: comfortable with good traction and no blisters. When we finish we walk to shady side of stadium, sit down, cool off and talk. My teacher tell me something that happen when he was soldier in my country.

On very hot day he go swimming with his friend in a river near their base. They swim to middle of river, then enemy soldiers begin shoot at them from other side. A bullet hit my teacher's friend in his head. Mr. Goddard grab the guy and swim with him to land. But he is dead.

It bother my teacher a lot because it is his idea to go swimming. Also the guy is his close buddy. After it happen, Mr. Goddard say he try not to make such close friends so he won't lose them and have to feel awful.

His logic sound strange, but as I consider, it kind of makes sense. It can explain something I wander about. Although he is high character person, Mr. Goddard does not seem to have many friends. Does he still stop himself from making friends?

*3/17/86*

Tina stayed with me for two and a half miles today with less difficulty than I would have liked. She seems to get a kick out of running. Soon she'll be happily running me into the ground.

We talked later. She told me about the crazy night she and her folks left Vietnam. Her dad had booked them illegal passage through a friend of his in Saigon. On moment's notice, ten o'clock one night, they abandoned their house and belongings and drove back roads with their lights off to Cholon. Had the police stopped them, there would have been no way to explain their luggage of backpacks and duffel bags. Inside was enough food, water, clothing, and medical supplies to get them across the South China Sea.

In Cholon, they joined Mr. Le's friend and his family for a clandestine ride to the river in a van. Their first sight of the vessel was numbing. Instead of the new ferry they'd been promised, they saw an old shrimp boat sitting low in the water, listed slightly to one side. Could it make it to Hong Kong, they wondered. They went on board to check the hold—absolutely packed with passengers.

There were good reasons to back out, but with most of their liquid wealth invested in the bookings, Tina's parents felt they had to go for it. Good weather had been predicted. They reasoned that a vessel which had stayed afloat so many years wouldn't likely sink in the next week.

Tina's last memories of her homeland are of that scary, confusing moonless night. A heavy fish stink filled the hold, almost choking them. After departure they listened to the anguished cries of those who'd discovered they left behind family members in the scramble to leave.

Tina and her parents went up on deck for a little peace and fresh air. They watched dark trees on shore slide past as the boat moved downriver through the delta. Tina wondered at the time—as she wonders now—would she ever return to her homeland? Then the captain ordered them below.

I thought she was going to tell me about the crossing, but she didn't. Changed the subject. I would guess she started to, then backed out.

*Tuesday, March 18*

Rayneece and Arvin return one hour ago. They arrive fighting, yelling at each other. She accuse him of putting scratch on her suitcase.

He drop suitcase on the floor, leave, slam door.

Rayneece so mad her eyes are big. She tell me Arvin take papers in his suitcase and work almost the whole time they are in Santa Barbara. Today, he want her to drive back so he can work in car. She lose temper and they fight all the way home.

Well, I see she's too upset to listen to me now, but in my opinion, she should think more careful. Can't she see Arvin needs all his time to work, so he can help Mr. Goddard win his hearing? Does she really believe everybody can take her fun attitude toward life? I'm sure Arvin wants to enjoy himself when the hearing is finish. He likes to drink, doesn't he? But now is time for hard work.

Maybe Rayneece and Arvin are too different to ever understand each other. Without understanding it is hard to keep a relationship. Maybe they should give up now, save all the fights and broken hearts. I just regret because Arvin is such a good guy—the kind of guy Rayneece surely need.


*3/18/86*

Arvin learned a lot from talking to his law prof, not all good. The worst is that the university tends to win about two-thirds of cases like mine, so the odds are against us, no question.

Prof found out the top floor of Administration is built like a fortress. He believes we're scheduled there so our opponents can screen the proceedings from public scrutiny, the better to railroad me. An open hearing would tilt the odds in our favor.

In a case of firing, he says, any CSU contract employee can request a public hearing. Of course I haven't been officially fired, but since the effect of my change in ranking will mean termination, we can use that to support our request. We're going to try.

After we went over what the professor said, Arvin asked some questions that floored me—all aimed at discovering if there's anything romantic between Tina and me. He seemed to be probing for a weakness. I guess he's anticipating dirty tactics by the other side and wants to make sure we don't have an Achilles' heel. I reassured him, I think, but not easily.

For the past several nights I've had this peculiar dream, another in the surreal mode. I'm in a vast sea of knee-deep mud, black and sticky. I'm slogging toward a red setting sun.

I notice I have company, of a kind. All around me eyes are embedded in the dark gruel. They are alive, watching my every move, blinking occasionally to clear mud. Thousands of eyes turn slowly to follow my staggering mud-sucking trudge.

I feel more exhausted with every step. I'm tempted to drop face first into the slick, cool oblivion. But the eyes keep me up. I don't want to touch them, not with the soles of my boots, certainly not with my body.

There was more to the dream, but that's all I remember.

What have we here? Paranoia? Not surprising I guess given my current predicament. But why do those muddy eyes make me queasy with fear even now that I'm awake?


*Wednesday, March 19*
Today a letter arrive from State of California. The state never write me before. Kind of surprise me. I open and find these few words:

THE PEOPLE OF THE STATE OF CALIFORNIA
To: Tina Le
GREETING:
    WE COMMAND YOU, that all business and excuses being laid aside, you appear and attend before

Three people's names come next—none do I know—then a room number: Administration 844. That's all, they don't even tell the day.

I realize this letter must be connect to Mr. Goddard's hearing, but what does it mean? Is it a letter they send because I will speak for him?

I phone Araceli to see did she get one. No, she didn't.

I phone Mr. Goddard, tell him, and he sound concern. He have me read the letter to him, then he call Arvin to see what he thinks.

I wait the whole day for him to call back. Finally he call. He say the letter means that at the hearing I will be witness for English Department, not him. Arvin is sure because he did not turn in his witnesses yet.

"Can they make me do it?" I ask my teacher.

"Yes. But it doesn't matter. You were going to testify anyway."

"Not for them. It's some kind of trick."

He say they will try to trick me anyway. And if I make mistake, Arvin can help me fix when he ask questions. According to my teacher, I will still be on his side.

As I think about talking in front of all those people, with my horrible accent (which it always gets worst when I'm scared) I feel weakness all over my body. Such feeling suggest I can't do it, I will fail.

"Still there?" my teacher ask.

Yes, I say, but my voice is weak.

Hey, you do fine, he encourage. Just tell the truth. Keep answers short. Practice reading "Minh and Dao." Practice in mirror, he advice. Practice on your roommate. Practice on me if you want. He say if I can read my story clearly at hearing, nobody in room will doubt I deserve to pass 002, 101, any writing course.

His words make me feel somewhat better. I will try to do what he say. Honestly though I do not look forward to this.


*3/22/86*

Araceli, Tina, and Arvin came over this afternoon to discuss the hearing, ask questions, calm jitters. Zane was invited but didn't show, so we started without him.

Went well on the whole. Araceli is really into it. She's itching to cross wits with the attorney for Cal State.

Tina's less enthusiastic. She feels like a traitor because she'll be testifying for the other side. She's wrong of course, and the situation can have advantages for us, but we couldn't get her to see it. We gave Araceli and her some sample questions to answer. Tina, throughout her responses, struggled with her confidence and her accent.

Male voices shouting in the hall interrupted us. I opened the door, stepped out to see what it was. Mr. Jazek, kitchen knife in hand, had Zane backed up against the fire hose next door. "Identify yourself, Buddy, or you're gonna get poked."

"I told you I'm a reporter. Stick me and see what happens," said Zane smirking, hands in pockets.

I joined them, explained to Mr. Jazek that Zane was my guest. He calmed down, apologized to me, lowered the knife. At which point Zane felt another two cents was needed. "You'll be talking to my lawyer, gramps."

"What a joke," said Mr. Jazek, glaring. "You think I got anything to lose?"

I steered our feisty manager toward his apartment. Arvin engaged Zane in conversation and led him to my place. Knifing averted.


*Saturday, March 22*
Today I visit Mr. Goddard's apartment, which I like it. It's on second floor with windows in every room. The light is very good. With the windows open breeze come through to keep you cool. Also the view is nice. Through livingroom windows you see trunks of four palm trees and past the trees is campus of CSUM up on hill. I imagine my teacher choose his place partly for such view.

His apartment is quite unusual in one way. It looks like some monk live there, because he have few possessions and no wall decorations. No posters, no paintings, just blank white walls. For furnitures there is desk, electric typewriter, book case, small TV, old sofa, that's all in living room. My teacher bring folding chairs from closet so we can sit.

In America few people wish to live like this and that's why I say unusual. But his home isn't strange to me. I am not American. I think the person who place low value on material things probably has high spiritual nature. And what's wrong with it? I am not really surprise to see my teacher live like this.

Rayneece stay in bed for three days—cry, play music all the time, just like I have seen her before. She hardly eat anything and she looks awful: eyes red, hair a mess, face miserable. If she speak to me, she speak like mouse.

Friday, she finally call Arvin. From what I hear, she make apology. And I think he make apology too, because she is saying, no, no, she's the unreasonable one, it's mostly her fault. I notice her voice is happy again.

Good for her, I think. She might keep that guy after all.


3/23/86

Last night's heavy rain woke me twice. This morning, as we ran, the weather was glorious. Clouds whiter than cotton sailed east, sometimes blocking the radiant sun. I guess because it's Sunday we were alone on the track. We set a comfortable pace and cruised. I have no idea how many laps we did.

Walking home, Tina gave me a Vietnamese perspective on the American moon landing in 1969. Her whole family saw it on TV, as did much of the world I guess, those with television.

Tina's father and grandfather, initially doubtful about the probable success of the mission, reacted to images of moonwalking astronauts with extreme suspicion. They decided the whole affair was an elaborate fake, paid for by the CIA and engineered by NASA and Hollywood. It wouldn't be difficult, they pointed out, to film cavorting astronauts against a blue screen, then transpose their images onto a carefully prepared acre of Arizona desert. The weird moon lighting? Electronic sleight of hand. The shaky, occasionally blurred lunar signal? Intentional distortion controlled by a random program. They had it all explained.

Tina said her mother accepted the reality of the event, but thought it useless. Anyone foolish enough to raise the subject of moon landings in her presence got the same blunt question: "Don't we have enough rocks and sand right here on earth?"

For Tina (seven at the time) the wobbly, brightly lit pictures were amazing, thrilling stuff. She felt certain it was happening and thought it wonderful. People were walking on the same moon she saw up in the sky. Everyone had always told her you couldn't touch the moon, and now....

The landing gave her a strongly positive image of the United States. Here was the America of big ideas and intrepid spirit she'd heard about but rarely seen in her own country. Even as an adult, Tina is full of admiration for space travelers, the astronauts, cosmonauts. She sees great significance in their quest. She's convinced that the perversities of human nature will eventually destroy the earth—so that our future, if we are to have one, must be out among the stars.

"If we're so destructive, why wish us on the universe?" I asked. "Wouldn't it be better if humanity died out?"

She smiled. "Universe big enough to survive our arrogance."

Didn't have a comeback for that one.


*Sunday, March 23*

Intellectually, Mr. Goddard is different from every English teacher I know. He argue in logical manner, develop his point with consistency, instead of use emotional arguments like so many. This make it interesting to discuss complex matters with him.

However, I do not understand why he is such big atheist. Everytime subject of religion come up, he take atheist position, even make fun of Jesus and God. Sometimes I feel he wants to shock me, because of course he knows I have religion.

What makes it silly is my teacher shows high spiritual character in his actions and believes. I see this in his way of living, his fair manner with students, the feeling he have for nature and animals, his political ideas. He just doesn't realize he is spiritual. My opinion? He should forget Christianity, which dont work for him, and look at other religions.

It is sad to know he has no believe. Even though a person lack friends, family, security, all the things somebody needs, the one thing most of us do have is God. God is the one who is always there.

*3/25/86*

The Grievance Committee turned down our request for a public hearing. They claim I haven't been terminated.

I figured that was it, but Arvin thought otherwise. He kept saying if we allowed the hearing to happen in ADM 844 we might as well not contest. His idea: to pack the hearing room with students, then negotiate.

"How do we get students up there?"

"Don't know yet. Not exactly."

Today at noon, an hour before the hearing, Arvin and I arrived at Administration to find the very students we needed milling in the courtyard. We talked to a few, learned that most had heard about the hearing through Zane's article. They came to see the action but had been turned away by cops. They weren't too happy about it. Arvin asked them not to leave. Said he might be able to get them in.

He and I took an elevator to the eighth floor. The doors opened onto four campus cops in a row. One checked our IDs against a list and let us onto the floor.

We walked around to scout it. The only other access was through the fire exit. It was locked, but not with a key. It had one of those twist locks in the center of the knob. I unlocked it and opened the door onto a concrete landing and stairway down. Perfect.

Our plan gelled quickly. Arvin returned to the ground on the elevator, where he found Rayneece had arrived. He had her begin sneaking volunteers quietly up the stairway. When they were all in place, he came back up on the elevator with an unauthorized witness (another volunteer). The cops of course couldn't find the girl on their list, so they wouldn't let her off the elevator. Arvin argued, and during this diversion I unlocked the stairway door.

Before the cops knew what was happening, Rayneece led a rush of over forty students from the stairwell down the hall and into ADM 844—which turned out to be a small conference room. Our troops packed it, filling the chairs, the floor, swamping the table with cross-legged and sprawled bodies.

Some used bicycle locks to attach themselves to chairs, table legs and each other. Talk about déjà vu. Of course, they'd seen old news videos and Hollywood films about the 60s. Maybe some had parents who protested. Whatever the reason, the correct spirit of excitement and happy camaraderie prevailed.

Roscoe Pennick, the lawyer for the university, arrived. He affected an F. Lee Bailey look with his dark blue pinstripe suit and dead-as-doornail eyes. A pissed-off F. Lee, when he saw the students.

The Grievance Committee appeared. All three were quite taken aback by the crush of smiling young faces. The hearing room was so crowded we principals had to meet in the hall to decide what to do.

Arvin stuck to one point, that the proceedings had to be public, especially in light of such strong student interest. The head of the Grievance Committee, who resembles an owl, hemmed and hawed as he glanced back and forth between Arvin and the student-crammed room. The other two Committee members watched wide-eyed. One of them looks like a Methodist minister and the other Humpty Dumpty.

Asking us to wait, the Committee retired to the President's office, maybe to consult the President—maybe just to talk in private. When they came out half an hour later, we learned we'd won. The hearing's been postponed to Thursday morning when it will recommence in RFK Lecture Hall, open to the public. There are about 400 seats in RFK. Just what we wanted.

Round one is ours, thanks to Arvin. And now we know for sure the University intends to dork me. Why else such enforced secrecy, with cops at the elevator and a locked fire exit? They wouldn't even let Zane in, a journalist for the student paper. Gestapo tactics.


*Wednesday, March 26*
There was much excitement at Mr. Goddard's hearing yesterday as I learn from Rayneece. I have to work and miss it. On Thursday, when the hearing starts again, I can go because Roberto will work for me.

Unfortunately, I make mistake and ask Roberto has he hear from any graduate school on his acceptance?

"You'll be the first to know," he snap, then walk away.

Maybe he's just nervous from waiting. Or maybe he's heard from some schools, but they say they don't want him. Will he likely brag about his disappointments? I don't think so.

He is doing well in Mr. Goddard's class. He show me his second CR+ paper last week, his city vs. country essay. That one was hard for me. If he doesn't get overconfidence, I think he have good chance to pass.


3/27/86

Page 1 of yesterday's *Student Times* was dominated by Zane's story of the hearing fiasco and accompanying photos. One picture was of happy, waving students occupying ADM 844. The other showed Zane being pushed back into the elevator by three cops, something I missed.

There's a sidebar announcing the time and place of today's proceedings. It concludes with a helpful tip: "Open to the university community. Interested students should attend."

RFK Lecture Hall was completely full when we got there. More than that. The doors at the back stood open to a crowd of maybe a hundred, barred from entry by campus cops but accessed to the doings by portable speakers.

As always on our campus, the crowd was dominated by black-haired heads, interrupted here and there by a gray, a blond, a brown, a red. The faces (as usual) included all colors of the human rainbow—from Senegalese ebony to Korean ivory.

The owl, Dr. Browner, opened ceremonies and introduced his two pals. Can't recall their names. The Methodist Minister is Dean of Music and Humpty Dumpty is a prof in Biology.

Arvin stumbled a little coming out of the gate, but soon settled down and delivered a solid opening. He laid out our position for even the least perspicacious to see, ending on this main point: "For five straight years the English Department's Promotion and Retention Committee gave John Goddard their highest ranking—a number 1. Excellent. This year the Committee lowered his ranking to a 4, which translates Poor, the lowest ranking. We ask a very simple question. Why the sudden drastic change?

"We will show that the lowered ranking was not a result of less effective teaching on John Goddard's part, or less publication than before, or insubordination as some claim, but rather his decision, in defiance of English Department policy, to pass two talented writers in a remedial course. We will show further that the policy in question is in conflict with the CSUM constitution, and that Mr. Goddard was therefore entirely within his rights to act as he did."

When Arvin finished there was silence for about two seconds, then applause swept the hall. Browner, lacking a gavel, had to stand and raise his arms to call for quiet. When he could be heard, he warned us: "Any more outbreaks and I'll have to clear the room."

Pennick's opening was wordy and oozed insinuation. He portrayed me as a rude, belligerent, wild-eyed Svengali. Claimed I'd duped some of my more gullible students into joining me in a misguided effort to overthrow the English Department and minimal academic standards as well. Though that's really all he said, his words droned on and on. I found his presentation cartoonish but perhaps the Grievance Committee was more favorably impressed.

I batted first for our side, as Arvin pitched me softballs. Took about an hour to go over my educational background, ESL training, publications, evaluations by colleagues and students—all the professional crap. We showed that this past year has been among my best in every category used by the English Department to measure professional achievement.

After that, the tough part. Since we can't dispute that I have been to some degree insubordinate on several occasions, we had to show that my insubordinate acts were, each and all, instances of political resistance to an unjust and inhumane writing program. Our problem was, almost every question Arvin asked was objected to by Pennick as irrelevant, and Browner sustained most of the time. We eventually showed some of what we wanted, but it took over two hours.

Arvin moved to my reasons for doing the grade changes. Went pretty well. Certainly we scored big with Article 113.22e. We thought the other side would know about it and have some B.S. cooked up to deal with it, but when Arvin read it out to the hearing, the confusion on Pennick's face (though brief) was priceless. I'll bet he spent one hell of a sweaty lunch break poring over the *University Handbook*, wondering what the fuck to do.

Guess he found no answer, because when he got his shot at me in the afternoon, he touched on the grade changes very lightly, the minimum. Just made me admit that in assigning the passing grades I'd intentionally disobeyed the Coordinator of Composition, the Department Chair, and English Department procedure. No mention of 113.22e. Most of his questions were aimed at portraying me as a rabble rouser holding sway over academic losers.

As I sat in the witness chair onstage I watched Pennick's words play across the faces of the audience. It warmed my heart to see how many people he was pissing off.

He moved on to quiz me about every argument I've ever had with Minter or the Hump. I was surprised when reminded how many there were. Unfortunately I hadn't told Arvin about them all, so he wasn't well prepared to deal with the damage. Our low point of the day—and my fault.

Pennick saved his nastiest work for last. He asked a shitload of questions about how I relate to my students. Do I get involved in helping them write their papers? Why so involved? Why do I work with them in my office? Why do I use individual conferences? Do I make friends with them? Do they idolize me? Do I use class time to present my political views regarding the English Department's writing program? Do I see myself as some kind of prophet or savior?

Arvin tells me I did well with these. I don't know. The students probably liked what I said, but the Grievance Committee? Most senior professors have minimal contact with undergraduates and think that's the way it should be. My involvement may seem suspicious. Pennick's portrait of me could appeal.

Browner adjourned for the day using the little gavel he acquired over lunch. With his woody beater in hand, he is more confident, more in control.

*Thursday, March 27*

Rayneece and me arrive to RFK Lecture Hall this morning and find whole place fill with people, every seat. We stand there wandering what to do. A police tell us we must leave. Then three nice guys make room so we can stay.

Arvin look good in his suit, so professional. He deliver a strong speech which wake up the crowd. For first time he seem like real lawyer to me. Rayneece is quite proud. I can tell by her face.

Next Mr. Penny speak, say a lot of mean things about Mr. Goddard. Even though this lawyer is impressable in appearance, I find he is not a nice person. Even his voice is ugly.

Then Arvin ask Mr. Goddard many questions. I learn things about my teacher I did not know. Example: he has Masters degree from UCLA, a top university in our city. He has publish many stories in different magazines, and he was vote by CSUM students as best teacher for 1983. Also, in four different years, his class evaluations by students are highest for any teacher in English Department. There was other stuff too, but I have to leave for class.

When I come back, Mr. Penny is asking unkind, sneaky questions while Mr. Goddard answer. My teacher surprise me by control his temper quite well. He did not get mad while I watch. Sometimes he even make joke, so Mr. Penny look foolish.

I know I can not speak clever like my teacher, but I must control my emotions like him when it is my turn. That way my mind will be clear.

*3/28/86*

At CSUM few classes meet on Friday, so we expected a much smaller turnout at the hearing today. Yet the hall was nearly full.

Araceli led off. Wearing a tasteful navy blue dress and spooked out in heavy makeup she ascended to the proscenium, crossed in front of the Grievance Committee (turning all three heads) and took a seat stage right. She pulled the mike down to mouth level and stared into the audience, wide-eyed, scared stiff.

Arvin's first questions drew her out on what it's like to study writing in an 002 class of mine. She was nervous through this part of her testimony and tended to answer too quickly, which made her sound rehearsed.

Then she read the first and last drafts of her strongest paper last fall—her city vs. country essay. In it she contrasts life in Mexico City with life on her family's small farm in Sonora State. Using her knowledge of economics and politics, she explains how commodity buyers and PRI bigwigs strangle rural life, making survival unnecessarily harsh, sometimes unbearable. As she puts it, "When city people say life in the country is awful, it is a curse they use their power to transform into human suffering. So much the worse for our lives; so much the worse for their souls."

As she read, the hall became so quiet it was like we'd all stopped breathing, caught up in the sad truth of her examples and the laser logic. She knows the paper is good and you could hear her pride. When she was done, applause rippled through the crowd, bringing more whacking from Browner and another threat to empty the room. Pennick looked like he'd swallowed a bitter pill.

Arvin's next questions concerned Araceli's failure on the 002 final exam. Pennick kept objecting, often with success. Our one clear victory was significant, though. On an overrule, the Grievance Committee allowed Araceli to read the final exam question out loud. Her delivery, slightly sarcastic, brought titters and some grumbles from the audience. On the faces of the Grievance Committee: purest consternation.

When Pennick took his turn with her, he started with a much milder approach than he'd used on me. But as Araceli's early answers fell short of his expectations, he shifted slowly into attack mode. Not wise, with her.

He began to ask about how much I'd helped with her city vs. country paper, and others. He wanted her to admit I'd provided heavy assistance, mainly through personal conferences. She kept saying, in different ways, the papers were hers, but I'd helped her improve them. The more he pressed, the more defiant she became, until she shot back at him "I'm just saying what happened, mister. Sorry it's not what you want."

Browner told Pennick to try another line of questioning. After some note flipping, he asked Araceli if I'd ever criticized the English Department in class. She said yes. Had she heard me criticize the final exam, the composition program, the Composition Coordinator, our Department Chair? Yes to most of those as well. But I'm not sure what it proves. Under any concept of academic freedom I can imagine, a teacher has the right to criticize the administration.

Pennick's last questions moved to a more personal level. He asked Araceli if I was her friend. When she said I was, he asked if I was her close friend. How often did she talk with me outside class? How often did she visit my office? Did we discuss personal matters in addition to schoolwork? Would she ever lie a little to help a friend out of a tough situation?

To that last she responded, "I don't need to lie. You do enough for the both of us."

Having gotten approximately nowhere, Pennick let her step down. It was past five and Browner adjourned.

*Friday, March 28*

At the hearing this afternoon, I write down all the questions Mr. Penny ask Araceli, write down her answer too. She speak well just as I expect, much better than I can. But the questions Mr. Penny ask her are not so hard. Tonight I prepare answer to every one, just in case he ask me too. These questions I can handle.

Tomorrow, Rayneece will listen as I read "Minh and Dao." She will tell me when she can't understand my accent. Then she will help me pronounce those words.

I must stop writing now to practice.

*3/29/86*

When Tina and I went to run this morning, there was a track meet going on in the stadium. I got what seemed like a good idea. Why not go to Griffith Park and run the fire trails? It's not that far and the views are wonderful. Tina was for it.

Well, I misread the clouds. Before we got half a good run in we were caught on a hillside by a thunderstorm. Took shelter in a eucalyptus grove. Very dark in there among those big, thick-trunked trees, groaning as they moved with the wind. For a while all we could see were the trees, the green hillside, and a solid moving wall of water. The city below was blocked out.

In that spooky environment my mind did a double clutch, taking me back to another rainy afternoon—the one Taglia tripped the mine in the chicken coop. I tried to save him again, as I always do.

Instead of tackling *him* though, I slammed Tina to the ground with all my weight, knocked the wind out of her. I guess she thought I was trying something. Had a panic reaction. Gasping for air, she flailed at me with her fists and kicked as best she could from underneath me.

That brought me back to reality. I got off her and stood, mortified. Slowly she sat up, trying to catch her breath. "Why?" she choked out.

I felt like an idiot, fumbled for a way to explain. "In my mind I went to another place completely.... I thought you were someone else."

I searched her face for help. The terror was receding from her eyes. She was watching me with cautious interest. I tried again. "There was another rainy day, in Vietnam...and I went back there for a few seconds. In my memory."

"It's a memory you want to forget, but your mind won't let you." Her smile was twisted.

She surprised me with that. I realized it didn't come out of nowhere. "Exactly."

"Yours are worst than mine."

"For your sake, I hope so."

She laughed, the tension broken. She let me help her up. "Sorry I hit," she said.

Dig. A 180-pound gorilla jumps her hard enough to break ribs, and she apologizes. But it's sincere. Losing control probably makes her feel foolish—so out of character.

When the rain lifted, we walked down the now-muddy fire trail to the parking lot. We were wet, cold and hungry. I suggested a restaurant in Los Feliz.

The rain came and went against the window next to us as we had lunch and Tina really opened up. She told me about the crossing.

The second day out, the shrimp boat's engine stalled. The crew got it restarted, but after that it stalled many more times, at unpredictable intervals, until it couldn't be restarted.

The next few days the boat drifted as the passengers used up food and water. Then a storm in the night swamped the craft. In the early dawn light, with the storm subsiding and the shrimp boat taking on water, they sighted a trawler—and sent up flares to attract it.

The seven men on the trawler, fishermen by trade, pirates by opportunity, boarded the shrimp boat and robbed its passengers. They searched in particular for gold and gold leaf, coin of the realm for refugees. One of shrimp boat passengers, maybe trying to protect his own nestegg, told the pirates Mr. Le was a Midas with much gold leaf hidden somewhere on board.

The pirates used a hammer on Tina's father to try to extract information he didn't have. He was beaten to death, his body dumped overboard. Tina didn't see most of the torture because she shut her eyes, but she says she can't forget her father's screams. They go on forever, in her memory.

When the robbing was done, the fishermen herded the women and girls onto the trawler, rammed the shrimp boat's hull, and sailed away, leaving men, boys, and grannies to sink.

The captive females were taken to an island. Mrs. Le died the first hour they were ashore. As Tina was being stripped for initiation, her Mom used a rock to bloody one man's scalp. Another man clubbed her from behind. Three of them held her down and cut her throat. Tina, restrained, saw it all. Why she doesn't have flashbacks as bad as mine, I can't imagine.

She was on the island many days (how many she didn't say). She became the slave of a man in his forties. He kept her tied up in a cave for his daily pleasure. Eventually she was rescued by the crew of a UN ship.

After she unloaded all this to me, I talked to her a little about Eddie. I find it's easy telling her things, almost anything. I don't know what it would take to shock her. She has seen the worst—had her nose rubbed in it—and when she was only seventeen. Kind of like me in that respect.

For some reason she isn't bitter. Doesn't hate any of those fishermen. I suppose it's her Buddhism. Acceptance of the inevitable laws of karma. Very helpful psychologically, I'll bet, if you can buy into the metaphysics.


*Saturday, March 29*

When I talk to Mr. Goddard today, I learn he is disturb because his bestest friend die recently, a guy he know in the war—Eddie. It bother him because he can never see Eddie again, never talk to him.

Of course he's upset, I'm thinking. Eddie's the one he speak with about things in his heart, his fears and secrets. But when I ask, my teacher say, "Oh no, we never discuss that stuff."

"Maybe you share same believe. Want to fight injustice in society."

"I don't know whether he was democrat or republican."

As we talk, I learn the things they discuss are only these: Vietnam war and sports. When my teacher say that, even he realize it sounds a little ridiculous. But he still insist Eddie is best friend, and the friendship is deep.

Eddie seem to be hero to him, the person who show him finest human behavior in every circumstance—even facing death. Eddie always know right thing to do, he say.

"Is stick up bank right thing?"

"That wasn't Eddie."

"Newspaper say Eddie."

"It was Eddie's body, and a crack-up mind."

"What happen to his mind?"

"I don't know. That's what I keep asking myself." He look at me, begging with his eyes, like maybe I have some idea.

I tell him he must talk to Eddie's wife and parents to understand what happen. Only way I see.

"Yeah, I'm going to." He stare at his coffee.

Then I ask about something that bother me a lot. I know I can
offend him, but ask anyway. "Why you never call your parents?"

For a long time he look at me. Finally he talk.

He explain that when he come back from the war, his mind is
very confuse. All he can think is the war and the things that happen
to him in Vietnam, depressing, terrible things. But now he find himself back home on peaceful ranch, where nothing much change and
life is safe and boring—so different from Vietnam. He feel like tiger
among chickens. Like nobody is safe around him.

Worse, his parents don't seem to like or trust him anymore. He
can see he lose his father's respect. His mother is afraid of him. She
won't even stay in same room with him, he say.

One night, Mr. Goddard go with his cousins to town to drink
beer. In the bar some guys insult him. They make fun of him for
being soldier, call him baby-killer, stuff like that, and there is a fight.
Mr. Goddard say he lose control completely, kind of go crazy. He hit
one guy so hard it break bone in his face, ruin his eye.

His cousins get my teacher out of there. They help him leave
town, so he won't have to talk to police. He take bus to Los Angeles,
find a place to stay with army friend. And that's how he start living
here 15 years ago.

Most of this make sense to me, but one thing I can't understand. Why don't he talk to his mother and father after all these
years? Can he blame them so much, even now?

"I don't blame them," he say. "But why should I call? Nothing's
changed."

"In 15 years many things change."

He remain stubborn on this. He does not want to call them, see
them again, nothing. For some reason.

I think maybe he is ashame to face them because of what he
did—get in fight and hurt somebody. I think he's afraid of their
blame. But you can't run away from such problem. It's bad for you
to try.

*3/31/86*

The hearing got underway this morning with several of my former students doing, in essence, testimonials. Arvin's idea and a good one I think. He got them to describe how I teach writing and what they felt they'd learned. A main focus was how I worked with them on their papers. Every student reinforced what Araceli said. I gave advice, but they wrote the papers themselves.

Those who spoke—Latrice Williams, Mara Escobar, Ricky Dang, Fatima Costa, and Razmik Kassajian—mentioned patience as one of my chief virtues. Only my students could possibly consider me patient. Yet, with them, it's true. Patience is part of the job, isn't it?

Pennick didn't spend much time in redirect with anyone. I think Araceli taught him the unwisdom of playing hardball with college students. And that did it for our side. Pennick's turn to call witnesses, and he led off with his ass in the hole: Fearless Leader.

Suddenly respectful in the extreme, Pennick spent a long time building up our chairman's credentials as departmental administrator and tenured professor of Medieval English lit. I suppose the purpose was to place Minter in a lofty ivory tower from which he could more easily spit down on me—an academic poor boy. But to my mind all the pomp and circumstance led nowhere.

I'm not a tenured professor, but so what? I don't have a doctorate—again so what? I don't need such incrustations precisely because I don't teach Medieval literature. The relevant question is, how well qualified am I to teach composition? Minter's powder-puff academic credentials haven't got a fucking thing to do with it.

Pennick next took our chairman through every little tiff I've ever had with him, probing ad nauseam Minter's spin on my bad boy antics. The portrait of me that emerged was of a spoiled Tasmanian devil, an employee from hell bent on shredding opponents and departmental decorum with his poisonous fangs.

For coup de grâce, the two went to work on my publications. Minter decreed that many of my stories were published in magazines he's not personally acquainted with. In my writing he finds a lot of "gutter language." My style: "hackneyed, derivative, and violent." Also, he noted that all my publications are creative. I've done no critical articles, no scholarly essays, no book reviews. He had me there, dead to rights. Never did no book review. Ain't got the smarts fer it, I 'spect.

It was almost noon, so we broke for lunch. Arvin and I ran to the cafeteria in the rain. We thought we could get some work done over food but barely had a chance to eat. During the forty minutes we were there maybe a dozen students came up to offer good wishes. Some I knew, others I didn't. It was great, very encouraging, but we've got to find a place where we can work. May have to bring our lunches and hide out in my office.

During the afternoon Arvin got his shot at Minter. He began by establishing that my professional credentials are excellent for a basic writing teacher. As good as anybody's in the Department. Score a big one for us, if the Committee is predisposed to rational thought.

Next, my evaluations by students. In the process of comparing faculty files, Arvin discovered my evals have been either highest or second highest in the Department every year since I started at CSUM. So he asked about that.

"I've learned to be distrustful of student evaluations," Minter said.

"Why distrustful?"

"Over the years I've noticed, all too often, the teachers who receive the highest ratings are the teachers who do the most coddling, who play up to their classes."

"So negative student evaluations would be the sign of a good teacher?" Arvin asked.

Fearless Leader looked uncomfortable. "Not necessarily."

The audience howled. It took some time for Browner to pound them down.

Arvin moved on to my publications. He got Minter to concede that my record is regular, extensive, equal to anyone's on faculty, including the tenured faculty.

Then he tried an idea of mine, sadistic but effective. He asked Minter, for the sake of comparison, to speak briefly of his own

171

recent publications, just to give the Grievance Committee an idea of what would be appropriate in this area for an English faculty member.

Pennick objected to the question as irrelevant. The Grievance Committee discussed it in low voices with their mikes covered. They decided that an answer from Minter might indeed help them evaluate my publications. As Browner explained, "Your department may have high standards regarding publication. After all, you're a language arts discipline."

Minter coughed, cleared his throat, face slowly reddening. "My responsibilities as chair have for the past few years precluded publication, though I keep up a vigorous program of scholarly research."

Arvin wouldn't let him off the hook. "Could you tell us about your publications before you became chair? For instance, what did you publish to get tenure?"

Inch by cruel inch Minter was forced to give ground until he divulged that in his whole career he's had just two publications. One a book review. The other an essay in *Medieval Studies* on Chaucer's use of tropes in "The Miller's Tale."

There were snickers, but no more than people could help. Browner let them die a natural death. End redirect. Fearless Leader decamped, looking whipped.

MHP came next, dressed for success in a snappy lime polyester business suit, charts under her arm. Her sparkling eyes knew something behind the bug-eye lenses. Her mouth restrained a smile. Hot to trot, she was.

In round one, Pennick took her through my acts of hideous insubordination, a tour lasting more than an hour. It was delightful to all who enjoy watching a horse being beaten slowly to death. Oh, how she relished heaping rectification on the head of the malicious teacher who'd so often thwarted her benefactions.

Round two shifted attention to the grade overturns. Here the testimony developed in a most interesting way, because Pennick wasn't satisfied with establishing that I'd defied direct orders. He also undertook an explanation and defense of the Humper's precious writing program, including the final exams. Occurred to me this might have been the Hump's idea.

Only minutes into her testimony, at Pennick's request, MHP placed her faithful writing goals chart on its tripod and began to lecture the auditorium like a corps of new writing instructors. The chart, a little dog-eared and faded, contains in block letters three words burned blackly into the minds and hearts of all writing teachers at CSUM:

VERBALIZE

ANALYZE

SYNTHESIZE

"Studies have shown," Humper began, "that competent college writers employ three main cognitive skills of increasing complexity. When students use English in an academic environment, they must verbalize, analyze, and synthesize."

She placed her pointer on VERBALIZE. "In English 001, our first remedial course, students learn to verbalize by writing their personal reactions to readings assigned by the instructor."

She moved the pointer to ANALYZE. "In English 002, our second remedial course, students learn to analyze by writing personal essays based on their comprehension of assigned readings."

Now SYNTHESIZE received the pointer tip. "And in English 101, freshman composition, students synthesize their personal opinions with those of an outside author.

"Thus, as a student moves through our program, he or she learns progressively to verbalize, analyze, and synthesize—becoming in the process a competent collegiate writer."

Someone in the audience groaned, prompting Browner to raise his gavel and scowl. But lord, lord, we were all groaning inside—weren't we?—especially those of us who've been through the Humper's cognitive skills lecture fifty times before. As teachers, we know the effect of her brilliant pedogogical theory on our classes.

English 001, 002, and 101 are basically the same course, for in all three the students do exactly the same thing: write personal essays in response to published essays. It's a boring kind of writing under the best of circumstances, made no less so by being repeated from course to course.

With Pennick prompting, Humper next explained the composition finals. She presented them as something of an educational breakthrough since they make the evaluation of student writing "entirely quantifiable."

This noteworthy goal is achieved by us teachers counting up every single error in every essay—each unneeded comma, misspelled word, misplaced apostrophe. All mistakes, from weak overall organization or missing thesis to one wrong verb ending are weighted equally at 1. The faults are totalled, then divided by the number of words in the essay. Five faults or less per hundred words passes 001; four or less per hundred words passes 002; three or less per hundred dicks 101.

This error-count system vastly overweights the importance of small grammar flaws because such are far more numerous than major mistakes. The overweighting disadvantages in particular students new to standard English, even those whose thought content is profound and original. Thought content counts only if there is an identifiable error—such as a logical fault. In that case, minus 1, same as an incorrect verb ending.

"Our use of numbers may seem cold and objective," Humper continued, "but it guarantees that the grader's emotions and prejudices are kept out of the grading process. Our system provides fair and equal evaluation of every exam.

"The final reading and final exam question are also designed to be fair, because they are the same for all students at a given level. We never have an easy test being offered in one 002 class while a hard test is going on in the 002 next door. And no instructors can give their students grades they haven't earned." She looked at me. "Until now."

By the time she and Pennick were through, there wasn't enough time for Arvin's redirect, so Browner adjourned.

Arvin is buzzed because he thinks Pennick opened a can of worms in letting the Hump defend her precious program. Now we can present testimony demonstrating the program is unfair, making it obvious why I had to change the grades. We'll be working on this before the hearing reconvenes on Wednesday.


*Tuesday, April 1*
Today Rayneece ask me why I don't go out with Mr. Goddard on dates and stuff.

We don't feel like that, I tell her.

"Then why you look at him that way?"

"What way?"

"Like a puppy in love."

Is she making it up, I wander. But she seem serious.

"How does he look at me?" I ask.

"Can't tell. He's hard to read. Likes spending time with you." She advice me go for it. Why not, she say. What you got to lose?

That was this morning, now it is night and I still consider her comments. I am so confuse it is hard to study. After all, what is my knowledge of love compare to Rayneece? Almost nothing. I am ignorant as baby.

Is she right? Am I in love with my teacher?

Well, he is my good and trustable friend. I enjoy being with him. I would say he is attractive man. But I do not feel strong need to marry with him or any of that.

He frighten me sometime because he seem to feel much pressure and can behave in unpredictable manner. In the other hand, he has high character and is quite gentle in his heart. I do not think he would ever hurt me. I know he wouldn't. The person in danger from his actions is only him.

He is not fake—not even a little. And he has courage. I would not want a weak man, that wouldn't work with me.

But does that mean I love him?

I am so confuse. Love for me I think will always be different because of what happen to me. I do not see sex as a wonderful thing. I do not know if I enjoy sex. Certainly I'm not consciously want sex with any man—and Mr. Goddard is just equal with the others that way.

There is one reason maybe I love him. I enjoy when we talk together, and it seem he feel the same. He listen to me so careful.
Usually he understand, because he is wise and knows about life. I
would regret losing him to talk to, a lot. But I don't know if that's
love. Even if it is, that doesn't prove he loves me.

If I act foolish toward him, as Rayneece would like, throw myself on him, I can lose him as my friend. After all, who wants
lovesick puppy hanging around? It is repulsive—unless you love her
back.


4/1/86

Dreamed a remake of a previous attraction. It's that one where I'm
swimming for my life on a vast sea, no land in sight. My whole body
is deeply fatigued, lungs burn. Feels like I've been swimming for
days.

I'm looking for something to cling to so I can rest. Debris bobs
on the gentle waves but there's nothing buoyant enough to support
me. I keep looking.

Underwater, my descending hand strikes and catches on what
feels like a bag of sticks. I can't shake it off. I use my other hand to
try and pull it off and that hand becomes attached as well. Though
nearly weightless, whatever it is clings to me like something living,
making it impossible for me to swim. I'm having trouble keeping
my mouth above water.

Wanting to see it I lift my hands, and out of the water rises the
shriveled corpse of an old woman, feather-light. Her long black hair
is laced with white strands. Her decomposed, eyeless monkey face
smiles a toothy smile. As I watch, her long long fingernails continue
to grow, sliding into the flesh of my palms again and again as they
curl around, stitching us together.

That's all folks. Don't know what to make of it really. Just re-
porting the facts.

Finished the Bierce letters today. They do get more interesting
toward the end, as he breaks off with those dearest to him. In the
last ones he's corresponding with two young women only—one a

literary protegée, the other a niece, sort of. His final farewell is macabre, brutal I would say: "Good-bye—if you hear of my being stood up against a Mexican stone wall and shot to rags please know that I think that a pretty good way to depart this life. It beats old age, disease, or falling down the cellar stairs. To be a Gringo in Mexico—ah, that is euthanasia!"

There have been decades of speculation about why Bierce ended his life as he did. Seems I've caught the disease. I see clues in the final letters that he may have been running out of money. Though he could always have earned more by writing for magazines, he remarked many times how he despised the sort of shallow thinking they wanted from him. And he was a proud guy—as proud as they come.

I'm going to collate his last letters with the end of his biography, see what it turns up.


*Wednesday, April 2*

I speak at hearing today. Unfortunately I am disaster. After Mr. Penny insult me, suggest dirty things in front of all the people, I lose control of my emotions, make silly answers. Worst, I begin to cry.

Mr. Goddard and Arvin think I did terrible. I know because after Mr. Penny finish with me, they talk together and decide not to ask me any questions. I'm sure they wish I didn't speak at all.

Can I blame them?


*4/2/86*

Arvin grilled the Hump all morning. Put the heat to her pretty good.

He asked mostly about the composition program, beginning with its record-setting ways. "According to the most recent *Bulletin of Higher Education*, which lists more than 5000 American colleges and universities, CSUM's writing classes have the highest failure rates in the country." Grumbles in the audience. "Were you aware of this, Dr. Parcell?"

"No. And I don't see the relevance."

"Were you aware that CSUM has the highest freshman/sopho-more flunk-out rate of all American colleges and universities?" More grumbles.

The Humper's eyes went stony. "The attrition rate will be high. We have high standards here. And some special problems."

"Special problems?

"Most of our students are not native speakers of English."

Sustained grumbles and one angry comment: "You're the spe-cial problem." Browner, with a frown, began rapping.

Arvin turned to the content of an article published last year by a professor in our Sociology Dept. She did surveys with sociology majors who'd taken English 101 at CSUM. Arvin put up a chart with the findings summarized:

ENGLISH IOI FAIL RATES

| | |
|---|---|
| Whites | 10% fail |
| Afro-Americans | 41% fail |
| Hispanics | 56% fail |
| Native Americans | 59% fail |
| Asian/Pacifics | 74% fail |

"Were you aware of these statistics, Dr. Parcell?"

"They don't surprise me."

"You see no problem with them?"

"Of course I see a problem. But it's no reflection on our writing program."

"Can you explain why the typical Asian student is more than seven times as likely to fail English 101 as a White?"

"Often the Asians, out of a false sense of security, live in cultur-al enclaves where only the native language is used. This makes them very slow learners of English."

"And the Blacks? Black Americans speak English as soon and as long as White Americans. Why do Blacks fail freshman English four times as often as Whites?"

"Not that many Blacks fail—notice almost 60% pass. That's

pretty good. And most of the ones who don't make it came to our campus writing in non-standard forms. They simply weren't able to achieve verbal competence in time."

"It doesn't trouble you that some groups have vastly higher fail rates than others?"

"We're not happy with the higher fail rates. But before we scrap the program, let's consider the alternatives. We could let the students write in Mandarin Chinese or in the ghetto dialects they're comfortable with. We could make the finals easier, so more pass. We could pass everyone carte blanche, on the basis that they're all nice people. And no problem—until those same students face the music on the job market. Their new bosses will find out soon enough they can't write competently."

"Araceli Chacon seems to be a competent writer. To say the least. How do you explain her failure on a basic writing final?"

"When a student fails who could have passed, the problem is usually motivation. I've read the final in question. That student clearly didn't take the trouble to understand the outside reading."

Boos from the audience, thumped into submission by Browner.

Arvin read from the sociology prof's conclusions: "Such wide differentials in fail rates between the various ethnic groups, with the culturally dominant group on top, is prima facie evidence of pervasive ethnic discrimination in the testing instruments, and in the testors as well, all members of the culturally-dominant group." He looked up. "How would you answer her, Doctor Parcell?"

"She'd be wise to stick to her own field, sociology, where she may be competent. She seems to know nothing about the pedagogy of writing instruction."

Arvin followed with the budget data he got from the Comptroller's Office in Sacramento. Forced Humper to admit that the high composition fail rates are generating big bucks for the English Department. That's because students must retake courses they've failed. The retaking of courses creates the need for more classes, which means more funding from the state, thus more power and prestige for the English Department. The more failures, the bigger the Department's profits.

These questions threw old Hump off balance, I would guess because she has little to do with the Department budget. Arvin had no trouble getting her to paint herself into a corner. By the time she stepped down, she looked ready to punch his lights out.

The afternoon didn't go as well for us. For openers, Pennick called on Danny boy so he could relate how he busted Tina for plagiarism in his 101 class. I was hoping Arvin would tear the old buffoon a new asshole during redirect, but for some reason he asked only a few vague questions, then let Braeme step down.

Pennick put Tina on next. He started by taking her through a detailed chronology of her "poor performances" in English classes at Cal State. He asked about her work in Ann Cowley's class and Dr. Braeme's class, then about the final she wrote for my class.

"Despite all these English failures, Miss Le, you did well on Mr. Goddard's essay assignments. Isn't that right?"

"I do better in his class."

"But can you tell us why?"

"He's a good teacher."

"Why do you say so?"

"Because he help me write better."

"Yes, but the question is how *much* did he help you? You and Mr. Goddard have a history of helping each other, don't you?"

Arvin objected. Browner agreed that the question was far too broad.

"By all means, let me be more specific. He helped you by changing your failing grade to passing, didn't he, Miss Le?"

"Yes."

"And he helped you in other ways. He gave you rides in his car, entertained you in his apartment, took you to expensive restaurants, walked you to very lonely places in Griffith Park and lay down in the grass with you, didn't he, Miss Le?"

Tina looked flabbergasted.

Arvin objected and was sustained, but it didn't prevent subsequent questions from Pennick about specific times and places Tina and I have been together, both in the company of other people and alone. Obviously they've had a tail on us for some time. There were photographs.

It was painful watching Tina struggle as she tried to stick up for me and our friendship. Naturally, she couldn't remember all the times we'd been together. Twice she denied a particular meeting till confronted by facts, then remembered and backed down. It may have looked like she was lying and getting caught. Pennick was certainly giving it that spin.

His last questions were the most mean-spirited and insulting. What kinds of things did she and I talk about when we were alone together? Had we ever kissed? Had we ever made love? Had I ever told her I loved her? Did she love me?

Of course Tina denied these, but Pennick kept harping, asking about our supposed romance in different ways, until out of sheer frustration, I think, she began to cry. But she cried only with her eyes. It was like her face was frozen and the tears appeared and ran down her cheeks. No one in the auditorium could have missed it.

Having got what he wanted, Pennick turned her over for redirect.

Arvin and I decided she was in no state to answer more questions. Also, any answers she gave would open her up to new interrogation by Pennick. Too risky, so we encouraged her to step down.

I followed her outside to thank her for testifying. I also wanted to apologize for not preparing her better. We should have anticipated Pennick's line of attack.

I've never seen her quite like she was then. She wasn't crying. But she sure wasn't happy. Seemed very down and noncommunicative. I don't know whether she was angry at me for getting her involved in the whole thing, or just depressed because it didn't go better. Maybe the latter. She tends to be hard on herself.

I'll give her a chance to think about it and calm down. I'll call tomorrow.

Arvin's closing was terrific. He had us in his palm the whole twenty minutes. When he was done the audience stood, clapped, whistled and cheered in a tumult that wouldn't be hushed. Browner's gavel had small power to intimidate as the hearing neared its end.

Pennick used his final remarks, predictably, to coat his previous character assassinations with an additional layer of slime. Took only an hour.

All over now. We wait for the Grievance Committee's decision.

*Thursday, April 3*

Mr. Goddard phone this morning to tell me how good I speak at hearing, much better than I think accordingly to him. I guess he feel I'm such a baby he must cheer me up with fake praise. His attitude make me so mad!

If you like the way I speak so much, I say, why don't you let me tell my side? It's not nice to have bad things said about you and not explain what really happen. Does he think I cant take it? Does he think I'm such a child?

He seem very surprise by my attitude. And of course, he start to apologize. So sorry, he say. We thought we were protecting your feelings, we thought you didn't want to continue.

"Can't you ask me?"

All he can say is sorry, so sorry.

I begin to feel kind of bore with our conversation. But for some reason he want to keep talking. He tell me what I already know, that Mr. Penny has no right to suggest those dirty things about us, to make it sound like we are in love, and worst. Mr. Goddard say he is furious that such suggestion is made in public, it can hurt my reputation.

I decide not to talk. When he realize I'm not answering, surely he will give up, I think. But no, I forget he is American. After long silence he ask another question. Is it true what Mr. Penny say, he wants to know. Am I in love with him?

I try to think of meanest thing in world to answer back, but I can't think of anything mean enough. I find I can't say one word into phone. So I hang up.

He call back, two time, but I ignore. Really, what is there to discuss with such an insensitive person!

4/3/86

Called Tina earlier. Our conversation didn't go well at all. I'm afraid I offended her—badly.

Can't believe it now. I actually asked her if she loved me. She wouldn't answer. Hung up in fact. But isn't there a fairly clear answer in that? If her answer was no, she would have laughed at me.

Christ, why didn't I see this coming? I guess it's because she's so nonflirtatious, somewhat asexual to my mind. I mean she's a beautiful woman, no question, but I never sensed any physical attraction between us. The way our relationship has evolved, we talk to each other, run together, that's it.

Did I in some way lead her on? In my need for understanding and companionship, maybe I did. But I didn't mean to. I'd never get involved with one of my students. Bad power situation there.

I'm not in the market for something like that either. How can I be when I know damn well I'm not safe to be around for prolonged periods? If Tina had been with me the night I went flying in my Mustang on the Pasadena Freeway, she'd likely be dead now or fucked up beyond recognition.

Oh yes, it would be easy to love Tina. All too easy, really. But it's not going to happen. I refuse to make Bierce's mistake of self-indulgent merging with the cherished other. I have no reason to think my love is less poisonous than his.

By the way, I was wrong about his reason for checking out. His publisher, Walter Neale, writes that late in life Bierce had plenty of bucks—savings, common stock, royalties and a lifelong pension from Neale himself. So poverty had nothing to do with the Mexican vacation.

Obviously Bierce wanted to go out on his own terms. Maybe we should leave it at that. Makes a great mystery. Best ever written by a dead man.

*Friday, April 4*

Mr. Goddard come to computer lab today while I work. He want to talk again, find out if the baby feel better. Also he want to apologize some more. Always there is that.

I find he has nothing new to say, and his presence irritate me. I concentrate on typing into computer and ignore him. After all, he is interrupting my work—shouldn't he know it? Soon, he gets the point and leaves.

I suppose this is old problem for him, foolish women losing their heads for such a kind, patient and adorable teacher. In the past there must be many like me. I am surprise he has not found out how to handle the situation better by now. He is so clumsy. Maybe he just doesn't care enough to do it nice.

*4/4/86*

Minter dropped by my office this afternoon. Smirking and without comment he handed me a copy of the Grievance Committee's ruling.

We lost on a split decision, 2-1. Only Chairman Browner supported us. In his dissent from the majority he agreed with our basic position: "The PRC's decision to lower Mr. Goddard's job rating so drastically, in so short a time, and without adequate basis, is clear evidence of retaliation." Some comfort in that, I suppose, but we still lost.

I called Arvin with the news. Thought it might get him down. Fat chance. If anything, he was more juiced. Tried to talk me into filing in civil court for unfair dismissal.

I said maybe, if I decided to fight on into the sunset as it were. But I explained my main concern right now has to be finding another job. It's already late in the academic year to be applying. I'll have to bust my tail over the next few weeks to have any hope of getting a decent position next fall. He said he understood, but I heard disappointment in his voice.

Tonight I feel drained. Need a few days to recover before I decide anything about anything.

Looks like I've blown it with Tina. Went by her work today and she froze me out. I seem to disgust her.

Nice going, ace.

*Saturday, April 5*
When I was little girl, I expect to marry when I get older, because I know most women do. Now I think the marriage state is not necessary for all people. Some of us can be happy without. Some of us may prefer to run our life alone.

When I finish school, I will probably make O.K. income, even if I teach. So I don't need no man to support me. And if I marry, how do I know he won't some day depend on me for support? Many women have it happen, I believe.

A husband can mistreat you, or run around behind your back with other women, maybe your friends. If you are not marry, there is no one to betray you and break your heart. And surely I have enough problems on my own, don't need somebody else's.

We all want a person to talk to, to share things with, because humans are social. But we can have friends for that, it doesn't have to be a mate. Certainly, without a mate there will be less complication.

*4/5/86*
Big day today. A day of despair and revelation.

After a listless, barely productive afternoon trying to pull together my academic resumé, despair filled me in the failing evening light. I was forced to realize I need letters of recommendation. Those I used for my present job are from grad school, old and irrelevant now, and the best I can hope for from CSUM's English faculty is silence.

I'm thinking, here I am, age 35, jobless, close to broke, about two-fifths nuts, addicted to alcohol and grass (maybe pills as well), nearly friendless, and without family. Can this be the same promising scholar/athlete who at age eighteen set off for war with fire in his eye and a song in his heart? Look how far I've come in seventeen years.

Puke tired with life, I fell asleep on the couch in front of the droning TV. Soon I began dreaming number one on the all-time favorites: "Vinnie and the Chickens."

It most ways it was as always: true to fact and hyperrealistic. Yet there was a difference, crucial, because after Taglia opened the coop, lost his face, died in my arms—and after I picked up his M-16, threw it on full fire and blew the shit out of those chickens, there was more, which I'd forgotten. The long lost second reel.

It reveals me searching the hooch next to the chicken coop. I find, in the floor, a trapdoor. Under that are earthen stairs leading down into a small bunker. At the top of the stairs rests the body of a tiny old woman with long salt and pepper hair. Her face, shrunken with age, somewhat resembles a monkey's. She's still warm, very recently dead. Below her right shoulder, her faded shift is soaked with blood. The way she's positioned—slumped against the stairwell, facing down into the bunker—she looks to have been hit as she was starting down the stairs.

There are really only two possibilities I see as likely: either she was caught by shrapnel from the mine that Taglia tripped, or I shot her through the wall of her hooch as I sprayed the chickens.

I find the entry wound in her side and feel it with my finger. It's the right size for an M-16 slug, but could be shrapnel. I look for the exit wound, can't find one. No answer there.

How could I have forgotten her?

Life offers many distractions to help you forget. My guilt over Vinnie's death probably focused me on him. Then there was the firefight that began a few minutes after I found the woman. I didn't get any sleep for the next two days. I suppose in the end you forget the things you have to.

So that's today's revelation. In adolescent rage over my friend's death, I probably killed an innocent old woman.

Burdensome knowledge. But of course it's been there all the time, eating at me from inside with Hell's own teeth. Granny seems to be the muse of my nightmares. Her blood, the milk of the guilt that's choking my life.

*Sunday, April 6*

Is it fair to hate somebody because they don't care for you like you want? I have been acting silly because I was hurt. Mr. Goddard can't help the way he feels.

Besides, he's my teacher. In my country it's not right to like your teacher that way. I can tell myself the class is over, he's not your teacher now, but still....

Today I phone him to apologize for my rude behavior. But I only get machine. I leave message: please call.


*4/6/86*

That old woman was somebody's mother...somebody's grandmother. Why did they leave her behind? Was she sick? Too old to keep up? Maybe she just didn't care.

Her position on the stairs, as I've thought about it, could suggest she got it from the mine. Because wouldn't she have started for the stairs as soon as she heard us outside, just before it blew? She should have been safe in the bunker long before I fired. Once down there, she would have stayed until we finished sweeping the village.

On the other hand, that mine was aimed away from the hooch. I know from the way Taglia got hit. Besides you'd expect it to be. That argues the old woman was probably safe from the mine—and that I shot her.

It's truly six of one, half a dozen of the other. Don't see any way to decide.

Can't stop thinking about it. Even numb on burgundy and Percocet my mind pores over the images it refused to face for so many years. Searching for a critical clue. Trying to prove me innocent—or guilty.

Tina called. I listened to her message record. She sounded almost friendly. But I want to have my head on straight before I call her.

Presently, it's not on straight. My short-term memory's shot to hell. And it's getting hard to focus on day-to-day activities. I carried the trash this morning and left the bag sitting on top of my car. Wish I could say why.

*Monday, April 7*

Mr. Goddard don't call me back. So this morning I phone again, leave another message.

Now it's night and no call. I guess he's disgust with me. And can I blame him?

Why was I so mean to a person who only want to help me? I was hurt, but can that be good reason to insult a friend? Now I maybe lose a friend.


*[undated]*

Something's happening here
not sure what. Mind
flying like a fucking
merry-go-rut, can't get
off, can't get off off!!
And that buzzing. What's
BUZZING? Please knock
OFF with the fucking
BUZZING, PLEASE!!! Whoa
baby, whoa whoa whoa


*Wednesday, April 9*

Today a police phone, Officer Chang. He say they find this man last night under freeway bridge. They think he got robbed because his clothes are decent but he don't have wallet or ID. Also his hands are cut, many cuts, probably by knife. The polices try to ask him questions but he won't answer. In his pocket is piece of paper which say "Call Tina," and my phone number.

Well, there is only one person I think it can be. I describe Mr. Goddard to Officer Chang. He ask me come to County Hospital to identify.

I take bus down there. It is my teacher all right. He is lying on bed with bandages on his hands. His eyes are open, but when I speak to him he don't answer, just stare at wall.

I go around the bed so I can look in his eyes. Still I can't be sure he see me, or hear my words. Only way I can describe is: his eyes look inside, not outside.

The doctor say my teacher have some kind of mental breakdown. At least that's what they think. They don't know how long he will be this way.

The hospital needs to contact Mr. Goddard's family. I explain it might not be easy. Can you help us, the doctor ask.

I say yes.


*Thursday, April 10*

How can I find my teacher's parents unless I have their name, address, phone number—something. And where will I find these? Must be at my teacher's apartment, otherwise I don't know.

Rayneece go with me last night. We talk to the old man who is apartment manager. When we explain what happen, why we need address, he let us in Mr. Goddard's place right away. Help us look too.

Finally, in cardboard box in my teacher's desk we find letter to him with postmark 1970. It's from U.S. Army and the address is in Kansas. Must be his parents address we think, unless they move.

The manager kindly tell us use his phone. Rayneece call directory assistance and get the phone number. She offer to call Mr. Goddard's parents—however, I feel I should do it. I know she speak English better than me. But Mr. Goddard is mainly my friend.

A man answer. He sound old enough to be my teacher's dad. I explain who I am, why I call. Unfortunately, he keep asking What? What? He can't understand me. He apologize, say his wife can hear better, I should talk to her. As he give the phone he tell her, "It's about Johnny, I think."

Mr. Goddard's mom understand me better. And she take the news well. She just say "Oh my God" once, and after that her voice maybe shake a little when she talk.

"Where you calling from?" her husband ask. I realize he is on another phone.

"Los Angeles."

"We'll be there tomorrow," he say, very definite.

But my teacher's mom isn't so sure. She suggest their son's mental condition is uncertain. What if they shock him with their visit?

She ask me what do I think.

Well, to me it seems my teacher's parents are sensible people. I don't believe they will make a big scene and bawl all over their son, like some. Sure they can surprise him—but is that bad? The right kind of surprise maybe will wake him up. Also, Mr. Goddard avoid them for way too long. In my opinion it is part of his problem.

I tell them come.

Now is late, almost time for bed, and I am alone with my thoughts. I have a scared feeling that won't go away. I am sick to think my teacher can stay breakdown, as doctor suggest is possible.

Tonight I burn money at my shrine and pray he get better. Tomorrow, I will do again.


*Saturday, April 12*

Mr. and Mrs. Goddard arrive yesterday afternoon. They come to our house in rental car, take Rayneece and me to hospital. John Goddard is just the same. He won't answer us, doesn't seem to see us.

Of course, this is quite upsetting to his parents. His mom have beautiful, very big eyes, and it's easy to see her sad feelings. But she doesn't cry, or say a word, just look at her son. Her husband put his arm around her. She take his fingers and hold on tight.

John's dad seem tired. He is quite large man, tall and strong-looking. His face is dark from the sun, but the top of his head is quite pale. You can see because he don't have much hair up there.

As they drive us back, Mrs. Goddard ask me and Rayneece about school and stuff. And we ask about their trip. We all try to act cheerful, like nothing wrong, but of course it's just a way to keep our minds off what we're thinking.

*7/10/86*

When I got cut up, a tendon was severed in my right hand. Required surgery. The cast came off yesterday so this writing thing is kind of an experiment. My index finger, still stiff, hurts when I bend it to a pen.

I'd like to record what happened during my mental lapse. But I don't remember a thing. Appears I took a little "time out" from life.

One day I woke to my parents' voices, pitched low. Couldn't believe what I was hearing. But there they were—seated next to the bed, older, definitely my parents.

Mom saw me staring. She stood, came over and put her hand on my arm above the bandage. Her hand was so cool. God how it took me back. All the way to childhood.

"How are you feeling?"

I wanted to say "I feel fine." But my tongue, swollen and tender, hung up in my mouth. What came out was something more like "Aw feee fah."

Mom didn't even blink. She smiled bravely, eyes welling with tears.

I spoke more slowly, trying to articulate. "I'm nah brain damay." I pointed to my mouth. "Mah tuh is swoe."

Once they understood, we all laughed. Soon three of us had tears in our eyes.

I couldn't begin to fathom how my folks had come to be there. I didn't know how I'd come to be there—with my hands sliced up and my tongue bitten nearly through. But it felt awfully good to be alive and have them with me.

Still does.


*Saturday, July 12*

I don't write in here for many weeks because I am too busy. Quite a lot happen.

In April, CSUM send letter say I fail English 002 last fall. Then second letter come, this time from CSUM Registrar, inform me I am ineligible student. After that my spring grade report arrive two months early. In every class I get: WITHDREW. So I am kick out of school.

Since I'm not CSUM student, I can't keep my campus job. Therefore I take job at bank downtown, full time. It is data entry position only, but because I usually work at least 50 hours per week, the pay is O.K.

I apply to several colleges for summer school. Best offer I get is Whittier Polytech. They say if I make C or better for English this summer, I can continue as regular student. So far, I have good grades in all my summer classes—B in English.

Araceli get NC for Mr. Goddard's class too, just like me. However, since it is her first fail in 002, she can stay at CSUM for now. We decide not to tell Mr. Goddard what happen. It can only upset him.

In most ways my teacher is much better. Just a few days after his parents come he wake up and start talking. Then he get out of hospital and go back to his apartment to live. Now he is fairly normal, except his hands shake sometimes and he is not quite as confident as before. He seem happier though. Happier and not so angry.

*7/13/86*

When I left County Hospital I began outpatient treatment through the V.A. in Lakewood. Part of that was seeing a shrink. The guy was a bit of a nerd, but he had insight. He helped me realize my main problem wasn't really the old woman I shot, or the enemy soldiers I wasted, or the buddies who died in my care. It was that I couldn't forgive myself for any of it. My self-persecution got so bad in the end that I couldn't live with the person who'd done what I did. So I snapped.

From guys at the V.A I heard about the Vietnam vet center in East L.A. I began dropping by. Went mainly for group meetings. These amounted to a bunch of us sitting around spilling our guts, kicking each other in the ass when necessary.

As I listened to the horrendous deeds some guys confessed, it in a way took pressure off me because my sins were put in perspective. A former LURP probably put it best: "Quit whining, you fuck. You were a medic. How many lives did you *save*?"

It's true. I saved a lot of lives. Far more than I took. Likely more than I could count. Anyway, the self-forgiveness thing, I've been working on it. Seems to be coming. Considerable indirect evidence of progress.

For one thing, drugs. I've cut down to a couple joints a day and three glasses of wine—max. Dumped the pills entirely. And fired Dr. John. As my head began to clear, I noticed his medical ethics suck.

The severe flashbacks are gone. And the bad dreams are less frequent and less frightening. According to everyone I'll have the dreams for a long time, but dreams are good, a way of working through the problem.

Been a change in my writing too. I scuttled Corporal Ernest Candide and his story. Lost enthusiasm for it. Started planning a different novel about Vietnam. I want to tell it all—the black, the white and the gray—with malice toward none, the way I view it now on balanced reflection. If I can manage that, I'll have something more significant than a comedic tour de force.

In talking with my parents, I discovered they never lost respect for me. They were in fact proud I went to Vietnam as a combat medic. Proud when I departed and after I came back. But they also worried. And when I returned their worry increased. Their gregarious, fun-loving second son had become a zombie who wanted to do everything alone. How could they not worry?

In those days, there was indeed someone looking down on me with abhorrence, but it wasn't my parents. It was me, projecting my self-revulsion into their eyes, so I could rail against the injustice of it. Another way of keeping hidden from myself the thing I couldn't face.

The parents' love for me is obvious. They rented a place in Alhambra to be here during my recovery. We see each other or talk on the phone most every day. Sometimes we take short day trips—like Saturday when we drove down to San Pedro, checked out the harbor and had lunch. Their concern makes me feel like the prodigal son. Here I exclude them from my life for a decade and a half, get myself all fucked up, and they treat me better than Gary who's back home running the ranch.

Tina's coming by soon. We're going for a walk around the neighborhood. Something we do once or twice a week. We may start running again.

*7/14/86*

I'd been wondering what kept Tina on campus so late. She wasn't home till seven some nights. She always had an explanation, but they didn't always make sense. Finally, last night, she told me the English Dept. managed to stick her with No Credit for my course. She's had to change schools. She says Araceli got NC too, but is still at Cal State.

It would appear my little rebellion didn't accomplish much, except to screw me and a few select others foolish enough to believe in me. There was, by the way, a final act in the farce. While I was in County, Zane Gorak organized a demonstration on the CSUM campus to protest my firing.

In tune with the times, the protest fizzled. A few dozen diehards got themselves pushed around by cops in the cold April rain. Some got peppersprayed. Two were beaten. Zane wrote it up in the paper to sound like the clash of the titans, but his story rang false. By then even he didn't believe.

I asked Tina why she kept the grade change from me—for months. She said she was afraid my knowing about it might set back my recovery, because I'd probably blame myself. Guess she feels I can cope now.

*Tuesday, August 12*

Last month this magazine in Maryland publish my story "Minh and Dao." That surprise me enough, but now guess what?

A letter come today from my Aunty Lan, who I have not seen since Vietnam. She is living in Chicago. One of her friends there see my story, see the names in it. Because this friend know our family well, she think the writer must be me. Therefore she call Aunty. Aunty contact magazine editor to get my address.

Aunty isn't sure it's me of course. But I will write her back. Maybe I can visit Chicago when I have vacation.

I also learn today that my new school accept me for housing. I will move to dorm and have new roommate, Ngoc. She is Vietnamese.


9/5/86

The parents are leaving for Kansas tomorrow. Took them out for dinner last night. Ling's Seafood Buffet. They *both* liked it. Might have made up for last week's great sushi disaster. Let's remember: as long as Dad can build his dinner around one or two fried staples, he's fine.

Back at their condo, Dad wanted a cigarette, so he and I went out on the patio. We'd been talking about me visiting at Christmas. Mom was in the kitchen fixing dessert, well out of earshot.

"Bring Tina if you want," Dad said, catching my eye. Then he looked away. He drew on his butt.

The offer surprised me. We hadn't discussed anything like that before. Normally such an invitation would come from Mom.

"We're impressed with Tina," he said. "Very." On subjects intimate, this, for him, was quite an oration. Embarrassed, he looked around for a suitable place to drop his ash. Finding none, he tapped it carefully into his palm.

Told him I'd think about it.

He seems to believe Tina and I are a number. Mom probably does too, though she must be unsure. If she was sure, she'd have issued the invite herself.


*Friday, September 5*
Mr. Goddard call to ask do I want to go for walk on Sunday? He suggest Elysian Park, where I never been.

195

Sure, I say.

As we discuss what's up, he begin to complain he can't find a college teaching job. In past few months he has six interviews for part-time jobs. He think they all go well, but he never get the position. Now he suspect his enemies in CSUM English department may be the reason. Did they put him on black list, he wander.

As he talk, he start to get angry. Since we have discuss this before, I've been thinking about it. I know they need teachers in high school. Maybe he can do that, I suggest, at least for a while.

"High schools are prisons," he say. "I'd be a prison guard."

"I think high school teachers like students better—same as you."

"I'd be teaching all day. When would I write?"

"Summer."

"I'm not qualify to teach high school. I must go back, get education degree. How can I pay for it?"

By this point I am thinking, don't tell me your problem if you can't listen to my ideas. But I know he is upset because he have bills. And he don't want to ask his parents for money.

Finally, when he has said every possible reason he can't teach high school, he thank me for suggestion. He say he check it out.

I don't understand his attitude. To me, the matter is not complicated. You need money, you must take any decent job you can get. Almost seem like he look for ways so he don't have to make up his mind.


*9/7/86*

Nice day today—cool, clear, breezy. Picked Tina up after lunch and we drove over to Elysian Park and walked the paths above the L.A. River and Frogtown.

Later we sat on a hillside in the park basin. Back and forth in front of us moved a fiercely contested soccer game punctuated by Spanish epithets. The sun was warm, but not too warm. Palm fronds high above rustled as their shadows moved on the close-cropped grass.

A capricious gust snatched a Dodgers cap from a young guy walking by on the sidewalk. His juggling recapture of the cap in midair cracked Tina up. She covered her mouth and leaned toward me. Her hair blew into my face. I was enveloped by the subtle but devastating fragrance of some perfumed soap or shampoo. Really it was the smell of her, amplified by the fragrance.

I felt weak—almost sick with desire, pure and deep. A knot tightened in my gut. Something I hadn't felt in many years. It shook me. My laugh was gone. I must have looked stunned.

Tina asked what was wrong.

"Pain in my hand."

Probably she believed me, but I couldn't forget what had just happened. I was realizing that, without thinking about it, she and I had drifted back into the same neither-here-nor-there relationship we'd had going before. Now, suddenly, I had the hots for her. Even my parents wanted to see us together, for christ sake. The whole thing seemed to be closing in on me.

I've talked to the shrink about Tina, more than once. He sees it like I do. Love thyself comes before love another; and forgive thyself comes before love thyself. I'm still working on forgive thyself. Would it be fair to tie Tina down when all I might be offering her is my dependency? And how could we get around the fact she started out as my student? To some degree, where you begin controls where you can go.

However, her friendship means a lot to me. More I'm sure than I'd like to admit. Never talked to anyone so easily as I do her—and we talk on so many levels. She's probably the best friend I've ever had.

I was thinking, maybe we could see each other a little less. Avoid the really long walks together, the perfect days in the park. Quite likely I should have continued thinking, instead of opening my mouth. But things were so balled up in my head, and my physical attraction to Tina so surprising and strong, that I wanted to get it straightened out right away.

We were going east on the Pomona Freeway when I began my little speech. Explained to her (who hadn't asked) that I wasn't ready to get romantically involved. Laid out all my reasons. Ended by suggesting we maybe see each other less.

Thought I was handling it passably till I noticed she wasn't looking at me anymore. She was staring at the backs of her hands, turned up the better to see them. Her face, very unhappy.

It occurred to me to ask her what she thought.

Waiting for an answer, I exited the freeway, decelerated up the ramp, hung a left onto Eastern and hit the brakes. The whole street ahead of us was clogged with stalled traffic.

Silence from the shotgun. Tina stared ahead at the traffic with a vengeance.

"Does *any* of what I said make sense?"

Her voice was cold. "I'm sure you're right about everything."

It began to dawn on me that I'd been, as usual, indelicate in my approach. Galvanized by that brush with her hair, I'd worked myself up into a lather—and then boiled over. What a colossal ass. And yet, I felt, I'd said what was necessary.

In time, the traffic began to move at a snail's pace. Neither of us spoke the rest of the way. I was afraid to reinsert my foot in my mouth. She looked super pissed off—yet vulnerable.

When she got out, all she said was "Good-bye, John." That's the first time she's ever called me John. And, to my ear, she said it dismissively.

She turned and walked to her house with a proud stiffness. Maybe she was crying, maybe not.


*Sunday, September 7*
Mr. Goddard kindly explain to me today he believe we see too much of each other. He is afraid we become too attach. He say maybe we can spend less time together, remind us we are just good friends. What do I think, he wander.

I tell him he's right.

What I didn't tell him is I think he is most ungrateful man on earth, most arrogant too. And I believe he has terrible weakness: he doesn't know the value of a friend. My schedule is busy, yet I always go with him, walk, whatever, nearly every time he ask. It's his idea to walk today. His idea go to Elysian Park. Usually it is his idea when we do anything. So how can he think I do it to trap him as my guy?

Yes, we can see each other less. He may be surprise to learn I can do without see him at all. Who needs a friend that every time you begin to get close to each other, he jumps away?

The guy don't know what he wants. And when he find out, he is scared.

*10/2/86*

Haven't had much luck finding a college teaching job. Decided to try something else. L.A. Unified is desperate for high school teachers. So desperate they've telescoped credentialing into one semester.

I applied for the program recently. If I'm accepted, I'll start taking classes in January. Feeling pretty hopeful about it. Teaching high school would cut into my writing time, but I can work that out.

I'm beginning to miss teaching. Writing all day is great, but when that's all I do, I get isolated. And I need the money of course. My story collection, when it comes out, can't be expected to support me.

*Sunday, October 12*

Aunty Lan call again today and we talk about various things. Finally she get to the subject she want to discuss: why don't I apply for grad school in Chicago so I can come live with her?

I promise, once again, I will apply when it is time, but it's not time. I remind her even if I'm accepted by Chicago, I don't know if I will go. Maybe another school will want me more—who knows? Naturally, Aunty doesn't understand that viewpoint.

Honestly, Aunty can be the most persistent and nosy person on earth. However, she can also be quite sweet, and I know the reason she want me to come to Chicago is so we can make a family. She is correctly thinking, there are so few of us left—let's stick together.

It is some weeks since Ngoc and I are roommates. I believe there is enough time to know, are we compatible? I would say barely.

She pays her rent on time every month, as soon as she gets it from her mom, and she is a cleanly person. That means she likes a nice clean room, even if she don't want to do it herself. Unfortunately, she is insecure. She always want to compete. It does not help that both of us major in math.

Also she has no sense of humor. Never a laugh, never a smile. Forever her face is the same, nothing. Sometimes I think she is trying to look intelligent, like math robot. Probably she can't help it though. It's just her.

Strangely, I'm better roommate to Ngoc than I was to Rayneece. To be fair I should act just the opposite. But it happens that way. One reason is I don't take so many showers now, so I don't make a big water bill. I take just one shower per day. At first, I did it for discipline. Then it became habit. Now it is easy.

Also I'm not so moody like I was. I think it's because, as time pass, I learn to accept what happen to me. My bad memories become less strong and I'm sleeping better. In result I am calmer person, kinder and more understanding to others. Ngoc may not deserve my kindness, but she is going to get it because that's the sort of person I wish to be. She needs a good example anyway.


*10/25/86*

A few days ago in the mail I got an invitation to Arvin and Rayneece's wedding—up in Fresno in a month. Great, I was thinking. Wouldn't miss it.

Yesterday Arvin called to ask if I could give Tina Le a ride. On impulse, I said yes. After hanging up I was flooded by second thoughts. I found myself wondering why Arvin sounded uncomfortable. I began to see Rayneece's hand in it.

I haven't heard from Tina since I told her how I felt on the freeway that day. I still can't believe how poorly I handled that, if handled is the word. God knows I've missed her. Yet it never seemed right to phone her, start things up again. I let it go.

Sometimes I wonder whether I made the mistake of my life. What do shrinks know about love, after all? And what do I know? Most guys would have gone for it.

With Arvin's call, I'm having to confront my feelings all over again. I would very much like to see Tina. But I don't know what her expectations are. Part of me, it seems, wants her to have expectations. Yet it still feels like she's my student. I don't think that will ever go away.

Given the strength of my feelings, wouldn't I be tempting fate to drive her up to Fresno, spend the whole weekend with her, drive her back? Especially if she's cooperating with Rayneece.

I'm beginning to think I'd better duck the wedding.


*Sunday, October 26*
This morning Rayneece call. She want to know has Mr. Goddard phone me yet.

About what?

About taking you to Fresno. Hasn't he call?

Then I see what she's doing. She's pulling the strings to get me and Mr. Goddard together. It's because of that day in the hospital when I admit to her I care for him. Since then, she won't let me forget.

Of course, it's true what I tell her. I do care. But also I think Mr. Goddard is right about us. His words hurt me at the time. And certainly he could pick better place to tell me than driving on street. But he was being mature and wise. When I consider, I realize I can never feel right with a man who was my teacher. For love to work, the two must be equals, both on same level.

Also, after his breakdown, he is not quite the same. He has much better mental condition, but his confidence and courage are not as strong. Sometimes he can have trouble making decisions. Often he seem to need my opinion, then he question my ideas. I still like him as person, very much, admire him too, but he is not quite so attractive to me maybe.

This is the part I tell Rayneece, so she stop trying to get me and

Mr. Goddard marry. And she understand. About why it's not so good for the student to love teacher—that she will never understand.

After we hang up I call Mr. Goddard. I want to explain to him, so he don't think *I* try to trick him. Good thing I call. He was ready to skip the wedding!

As we discuss, we decide it's no big deal if he take me to Fresno. We're both adults. It will let us catch up on what we been doing. Also, I want to give him a calmer image of me than he see last time. I want him to remember me like I really am.

As I now believe, the strong feelings I have for my teacher are most fortunate, because they show me I can love and trust a man. For many years I did not know how to love or trust anyone, especially men. It is the greatest thing my teacher teach me, and surely this is the purpose of my love for him.

There are many kinds of love in the world. And which kind is best? Maybe I can answer by the time I die.

In the end, what you have is memories. And I believe the most you can hope is more good memories than bad ones. Memories that never fade away if they happen when you are young, full of the pain and joy of being alive.